The Night Heroes:

When Serpents Rise

The Night Heroes:

When Serpents Rise

Dr. Bo Wagner

Word of His Mouth Publishers
Mooresboro, NC

All Scripture quotations are taken from the **King James Version** of the Bible.

ISBN: 978-1-941039-98-4
Printed in the United States of America
© 2016 Dr. Bo Wagner (Robert Arthur Wagner)

Word of His Mouth Publishers
Mooresboro, NC
www.wordofhismouth.com

Cover art by Bo and Dana Wagner

The power of prejudice was as subtle and persuasive as ever, and apparently, I was living proof of that. But now that I knew better, could this disaster be stopped? I looked out the window of the tiny cabin up on the hill and could see movement in the trees down below. The Pit Viper and his posse were heading this way, and if history were a good indicator, they would not be taking any prisoners, including us. From the back of the room, I could hear Rain Water moaning. He was in no shape to fight and no shape to run.

"We have company coming, guys," I said to Carrie and Aly, "and I don't think they're bringing house-warming gifts."

If we were lucky, this would be a very long day. If we were not, we might not live long enough to see tomorrow.

Chapter One

Boy, oh boy, it is hard to imagine a better way to start a week! This was one of those rare treats for us Warner Kids, a chance to be somewhat normal for a change, though with us, "normal" is a highly relative term. My sisters and I are PKs, preacher's kids. Specifically, our dad is an evangelist. This results in a highly unusual lifestyle for us kids. Dad travels all over the country and much of the world preaching, and mom and we kids come right along with him. Our school is done in the vehicle, or in a hotel room, or in a church Sunday school room, wherever we happen to be. We only see home a handful of times a year.

None of us mind, not in the least. We get to travel the world seeing God's amazing creation, meeting some of the nicest people you could ever imagine, and seeing lots of lost people come to know Christ as their Savior. It is an unusual life, yes, but we love it.

But that does not end the "unusualness" for us, not by a long shot. You see, my sisters and I are also special, very special. We (Kyle, Carrie, and Aly Warner) are the Night Heroes.

If you have read any of our other books, you already know what that means. But maybe you haven't read them, so let me catch you up to speed if you haven't. When my dad goes to preach somewhere, my sisters and I are often awakened in the night by the voice of the Conductor. We call him that because the first time it happened, he was a train conductor in West Virginia of the year 1912. When he calls, we wake up sometime and somewhere in the past. It always seems to have some tie-in to where we are and what we see during the day.

God uses him to send us on missions for Him in the past. When the day is done, if we are not being held captive somewhere, we go to sleep and then wake up back in our time just as fully rested as if we had gotten a complete night's sleep. We can take whatever we go to sleep with back in time with us, and that has proven to be exceptionally handy.

We have rescued a little boy from bad men in the mine, helped a little girl escape from a concentration camp in Nazi Germany of World War II, kept two brothers from killing each other during the Battle of Chickamauga, faced off against a knife wielding Indian, and dealt with a pirate off the coast of North Carolina.

Like I said, "unusual." But that brings me right back to this, one of the few weeks of the year that we get to be "normal." This is not a revival week for us; it is a week of camp! Our home church youth group is going to Camp Hosanna in Hiawassee, Georgia, and mom and dad are the ones taking all of us down there since he will be preaching. That helps our pastor out and gives us some great time just to be regular hyper, goofy, fun-loving kids.

And there is a pile of us. It is we three Warner kids plus Mari, Kandy, Melinda, EJ, Nolan, Sarah, Donnie, and a new guy named Drew. Everyone else we have known for years; Drew just got to church a couple of weeks ago. But since we have been gone in meetings for the past several months, this would be our first time meeting him.

Dad wheeled the trusty old Yukon into the church parking lot, and we saw the other kids and their parents waiting for us. Dad let us out, parked, then went over to the church van to check and make sure the luggage trailer had been properly hooked up to it.

The next few minutes were all high fives, fist bumps, hugs (the girls, not me), and catching up with all of our friends. It is good to have Christian friends; no matter how long you have been gone, it seems like you were just together a few minutes ago.

"Hey, Kyle," EJ said with a decidedly southern drawl, "this here is Drew; he started coming a few weeks ago."

I pivoted left just a bit and stuck out my hand to a kid fully two inches taller than me. That was not at all a normal thing; I just turned fifteen and am already exactly six feet tall and strong as a bull.

"Hey, Drew, nice to meet you."

"Yeah, it is nice to meet yuse guys as well," he said as he shook my hand and nodded toward my sisters.

Yuse guys? What in the world! This kid had an accent straight from the heart of Brooklyn.

I don't know why, I really don't, but for some reason, I instantly felt myself not liking this guy. He had a crooked smile that looked very much like a smirk, his hair was slicked straight back and was greased down, and he was wearing a black leather jacket.

In the summer. Eighty-degree weather.

I have dealt with a lot as a Night Hero, and I believe I am a fairly decent judge of character by this point. This guy was nothing but trouble with a capital "T."

We still had our handshake going, so just to send a message to him that trouble would not be tolerated, I squeezed. Hard.

His eyes widened a bit, then narrowed to angry slits, and he squeezed back just as hard. For a second, everything was quiet.

"Um, everything okay, guys?" Mari asked.

"Just fine, no problem at all," I said with a smile.

We released our grips, and everybody started picking up pieces of luggage to put in the trailer. Naturally, there were approximately three pieces of girl luggage for every one piece of guy luggage.

"Um, Bro," Aly asked as she sidled up to me, "what exactly was that about?"

"What do you mean, Squirt?" I said innocently.

"You know exactly what she means, Kyle," Carrie said with obvious concern in her voice as she moved to stand in front of me. "You treated Drew like he is an enemy or something. That is as unfriendly as I have ever seen you during daytime hours!"

I have to admit, I instantly got a bit irritated with her.

"Look, Carrie, I'm not exactly a normal fifteen-year-old."

"No, and I'm not a normal fourteen-year-old and Aly isn't a normal twelve-year-old. What does that have to do with anything?"

"I just don't like him. Don't ask me to explain it; it's just a gut feeling right now, but that guy is going to be an issue, and I intend to let him know that I won't allow it."

"Good grief," Aly said with a disgusted huff, "I think your testosterone is tap dancing on your good sense. You don't even know the guy; settle down and give him a chance."

The next few minutes? Well, I am not going to go into tedious details, but my sisters and I had a rather heated, whisper and hiss back and forth kind of argument that really started what should have been a pleasant week off on a very unpleasant tone.

I really hated that, but they were being completely unreasonable. After all we have been through together, they should know to trust me by now.

Within a short and hectic few minutes all of the luggage was loaded, all of us kids were in the van, and dad was praying as we prepared to leave.

"Lord," he said earnestly, "Thank You for the opportunity to go to camp with these precious kids. Please be with me as I drive, the cargo is too precious for me to be careless. Be with the van, let it run well. Protect us all the way there, all the while that we are there, and all the way back. Help me as I preach, let me be filled with the Holy Ghost, let many souls be saved, and let the heart of every Christian be challenged to greater devotion to You. These things I pray in the matchless name of Jesus, amen."

And with that, Dad and the kids up front were looking out of the windshield as the bus moved out, and everyone from the second row back was already talking, laughing, joking, and discussing all that they would do down at Camp Hosanna.

Me? I was staring at the back of a greasy head of hair, getting angrier by the moment. This week was not starting off well for me, not by a longshot.

Chapter Two

Once my irritation level settled down from a 9.5 to somewhere around a 6, the rest of the trip down to Camp Hosanna was relatively uneventful.

The mountains of North Georgia are a beautiful thing; a rare gem cut and fashioned by the hand of our good God. The road we were on followed the path of the valley buried deeply among the mountain peaks, winding back and forth, curving around lakes, jaunting over rivers. It was a constant barrage of green, as the trees were as thick as carpet, and all crowding against one another fighting for what sunlight was available to them.

A couple of times along the way we had to stop for a bathroom break. That many teenagers sloshing full of Mountain Dew and iced tea, laughing and giggling, never make it too far without someone realizing his or her bladder is about to burst.

Four hours after we left the church, dad whipped the van and trailer left onto Swallow's Creek Road, then in a few seconds took a right onto Pope Road, and a few bumpy seconds later we were pulling up in front of the office.

If anyone was expecting a leisurely, take a few moments and get acclimated kind of greeting, they would be disappointed. As soon as the van came to a stop, a huge group of banner waving, top of the lung screaming, running and jumping counselors came out to meet us. Our heads were spinning as they chanted and cheered, grabbed our luggage, slapped us on the backs, and started introducing themselves: Josh, Zach, Dylan, Matt, Gavin, Austin, Garret, Savannah, Haley, Lisa, Esther, Jenny, Quincey, Mackenzie, and Amber. These would be our cabin staff for the week, our counselors and guides to all things Camp Hosanna.

The girls all immediately fell in behind a live wire, hyper blonde with a million-watt smile. My head was still spinning from all of the names being shouted and thrown around, but I remembered that she was the one named Quincey. We guys fell in behind a wiry, athletic, close shaved guy named Josh. From there it was a crazy, luggage-toting, all out running, breakneck dash for the cabins all the way across the open playing field. People tripped and fell, quickly jumped up and continued the mad dash, hooped and hollered, and about thirty seconds after the run started, we burst through the doors of our sleeping quarters for the week.

The girls would be in six cabins to the left of the bathhouse; the boys would be in six cabins to the right of the bathhouse. Mom and dad, after they got us all signed in, would be heading for a lovely two-story house on the corner, overlooking the property. They would have air conditioning, a refrigerator, and privacy. As Aly would say, "Lucky!"

We did not stay in the cabins for long. Turns out "down time" is not in Camp Hosanna's vocabulary, nor is it in the vocabulary of Stan and Spring Wood who, thankfully, got the burden to start the camp and still oversee it behind the scenes.

We found ourselves rushing/being herded out onto the open field pretty quickly. The entire camp is in a flat valley surrounded in the distance by the lovely Georgia mountains. Serving as a barrier to the camp on two sides is an amazing mountain stream. It is pretty wide as streams go, deep in spots, and as my dad would say, "as cold as a kiss from Judas Iscariot."

It didn't take long for a good old-fashioned game of football to break out. We guys tended to that, and the girls all headed for the multiple volleyball courts. For the next

17

couple of hours, the girls served and hollered and volleyed and laughed and spiked and giggled and screamed and hollered some more. We guys engaged in an utterly epic game of no holds barred, no blood no foul, tackle anything that moves kind of football.

All the while there was some smiling lady circling the field with a funny contraption on her head. She did that both for the guy's football and the girl's volleyball. It finally clicked with me that she was taking pictures with a GoPro. I found out later on that she is Mrs. Kelli Graves. If she took one picture that week, she had to have taken at least 10,000!

Late in the afternoon we had supper. The supper hall is actually the meeting hall as well. It is an open air arbor, with a kitchen and office on one end, restrooms on the other, and room for a couple of hundred people to sit in the middle.

One thing we quickly found out about Camp Hosanna: the food is off-the-charts good, and there is plenty of it. The camp director, Brother Bill Abbott, has decreed that the standard camp food fare (possum casserole, ooey-gooey-uppy-chucky, etc.) will not do for Camp Hosanna. About the only place I have ever eaten better is anywhere that my mom does the cooking.

We ate, we talked, we laughed, and sometimes we actually remembered not to do all of that at the same time. Oh, and there were some really, really cute girls there! Hey, I'm fifteen, did you expect me not to notice that?

Anyway, we had a blast at supper. But pretty quickly, Brother Abbott (who is also an evangelist, and a really, really good one) got everyone away from the tables and started getting his staff to set everything up for the night service.

And man, what a service!

We had some games and skits first, and I about laughed my head off. I looked over at Carrie and Aly from time to time, and I could tell they were enjoying themselves just as much.

But all of the silliness soon gave way to the really important stuff, the preaching time. I could see something in my dad that no one else but we in his family would be able to see: he was very nervous as he started. Not because of stage fright or anything like that. Dad always gets nervous when preaching to young people, because he knows how important every single one of them are to God, and he never wants to be anything less than perfect in the way he preaches or ministers to them.

No one else would see that, but I did. So as he began, I silently said a prayer for him. It seemed like the least I could do; I know that he stays up late into the night praying for my mom and my sisters and me.

He did a great job, I think. He preached his message from Genesis 24 on *How to Find the Right Mate*. That one certainly made for a good ice breaker! We laughed a lot during that message, young people always do. Dad really acts pretty silly in it at times, but it gets the point across.

That night, something happened that I have learned not to be surprised at. Even though it was not a salvation message, a girl got saved. You see, Brother Abbott and all the camp staff and all of the great folks at Mt. Zion Baptist Church there in Hiawassee, had been praying for this week of camp for over a year. Combine that with any accurate preaching of God's Word, and you have a recipe for the power of God to fall. Man, I just love it when someone gets saved! I was walking on clouds, feeling like I was about to go to heaven while still alive and wide awake.

And then I saw it – Drew, sitting near the back, arms folded, still wearing that black leather jacket in the heat of the muggy Georgia night.

What in the world is it about personal conflicts that can make a person who has just been rejoicing in the things of the Lord turn as sour as a persimmon in about one one-millionth of a second? My dad often says that the filling of the Spirit seems to be one of the easiest things for the devil to snatch from us, not because of any lack of power on the Holy Spirit's part but because of a decided lack of focus on our part.

Thinking of that truth, I turned away and made my way to a corner of the altar to pray. I begin to pray that God would expose Drew for the troublemaker that I was sure that he was, and that he would give me the wisdom and the strength to know how to deal with him.

You know, normally when I pray I have a really easy time feeling as if I've gotten an audience with God Himself. But for whatever reason, as I knelt there in prayer earnestly pouring my heart out to God, it sure felt like the heavens were brass, and that my prayers were bouncing off of them and raining back down on my head. Could that guy be such a bad influence that he was even affecting my prayer life? I remembered that Daniel had his prayers hindered by spiritual enemies; maybe that's what was happening to me as I knelt to pray.

After a few frustrated minutes, I gave up, got up, and went back to my seat. The service was winding down anyway, and Brother

Abbott was giving us some words before we dismissed.

Our counselors broke us up into smaller groups by our cabin groupings, and we went off to different areas of the open field have to some devotion time with just our cabin mates. I was really glad that Drew was in another cabin; I really needed to get that distraction out of my mind so I could feel like I was right with the Lord again.

We had a really good time testifying, reading some Scripture, and then taking prayer requests and praying for them. By that time, the dominant light was the lovely moon raining the reflection of the sun down onto the open field. Each time see that I'm reminded that the moon has no light of its own; it is merely a reflector of the light of the sun, and if it isn't reflecting that light, it isn't doing its job. That is the way we as Christians are supposed to be, reflectors of the light of the S O N. So as we made our way quietly across the field to our cabin to go to sleep for the night, I prayed that God would help me to be a reflector of His light.

Those heavens of brass? They were still firmly in place.

Chapter Three

There are a lot of time-honored traditions at camp. One of those traditions is that people torment each other during the night. A couple of guys will stay awake, pick out someone else, and then do something charming like putting shaving cream in his hand and tickling his nose with a feather, resulting in the victim slathering shaving cream all over his own face.

I was prepared for this and any other number of typical practical jokes. What I was definitely not prepared for was having somebody grab me by the fabric on my T-shirt around my neck and shake me furiously. That, friend, was way over the line, and my eyes immediately snapped open ready to surprise somebody with a good old-fashioned chewing out.

Turns out, I was the one about to be surprised. What in the world was Carrie doing in the guy's cabin shaking me in the middle of the night?

"Get up, Kyle," she hissed, "get up now!"

"What in the world has gotten into you? For goodness sake, go back to your cabin and go to sleep before somebody sees you!" I hissed back.

"That's not going to be possible right now, Kyle, so I'm going to say it again, get up!"

And that's when it hit me. There was rock under my back, not a mattress. There was no moonlight shining in through the cabin window, but there was the unmistakable flicker from the flame of a torch landing on stone walls.

Immediately I jumped to my feet, looking all around me, taking in the surroundings. There was Aly, about ten feet away, leaning up against the wall with her arms crossed and an only slightly amused look on her face.

"Welcome to wherever, whenever, big brother."

I shook my head slowly and then put it down just a bit into the palm of my hand.

"Well, this never crossed my mind, what about you guys?"

"No," Carrie answered matter-of-factly, "it most certainly did not."

"No, me either," Aly said.

"Well, it appears that we aren't exactly going to get a normal week of camp like the other kids."

As I said it, I could actually hear the wallowing self-pity in my voice. Apparently, I wasn't the only one that heard it. From a dark corner of the cave that the light had not shown into came the unmistakable voice of our trusted guide, the Conductor.

"Is normal what you really want, Kyle? If normal is what you want, normal is what God will give you. But if you want something more than normal, you must know by now that it will come with great responsibility. But after all of the adventures you have been sent on thus far, you should also remember that great responsibility also comes with great reward. You have been places and seen things and done things that other people can only dream about. Perhaps you should be just a touch more grateful that God has chosen to bless you with one more opportunity to serve Him by serving others."

Ouch.

But he was right, completely right, and I knew it.

"I apologize, sir, that was really inappropriate of me. We can have a great week of camp just like everybody else, and in the meantime, we get the privilege of doing whatever it is God wants us to do in this time. None of us take that lightly, and I would like to apologize for my complaining and bad attitude."

The Conductor smiled with infinite kindness, and I knew that all was forgiven.

"Well, Carrie, this would normally be the time that I have you look around, evaluate the surroundings, and see if you can determine where and when we are. But seeing as how we are in a cave, and our entire surroundings are only about fifteen by fifteen, that may be a bit difficult for you to do."

"Maybe, maybe not," Carrie said as her eyes grew wide. "Look!"

As she said that, she pointed the torch toward the very back wall of the cave. The fact that she and I and Aly all let out a small gasp was not nearly as surprising as the fact that our Conductor did as well. Let me tell you, that really did surprise me! Apparently, he did not know about these clearly ancient drawings and paintings on the wall of the cave.

"Wow, just wow," Aly said. "What in the world do you make of this, Carrie?"

It didn't bother me in the least that my youngest sister asked Carrie instead of me. If you've read any of our adventures, you know that Carrie is the resident genius of the team. She absorbs information like a sponge and never seems to miss anything.

Carrie, though, for her part, was not saying anything yet. She was looking at the symbols, and I knew that she was memorizing them. But after two or three minutes of silence, she turned to us and said, "Guys, I have literally no idea what any of this means. It's not like anything I've ever seen in person or even in books. The one thing I can tell you is that the center symbol is easy to recognize: it is a serpent, rising from an ash pile, and oddly enough a blue ash pile, the only blue on the entire wall. I don't know what that means, but something tells me it's probably not good."

We all turned to look at the Conductor, and the mixture of concern and confusion on his face told us that he didn't know any more than we did about the meaning of the symbols.

"Night Heroes, all I know at this point is the general reason you are here. The year is 1780, and you are obviously still in the mountains of North Georgia, not many miles or so from where you will be at camp during the day. This small cave we are in is near the top of Hightower Bald Mountain, which stands 4,568 feet tall. There is a small town down in the valley. You can find it by descending the mountain and going about a mile down the Unicoi Trail. When the sun rises in just a few moments, you need to go down to that town. There is trouble brewing, and God has sent you there to deal with it."

"Pardon me, sir, but that is a lot more vague than the instructions we are normally given."

"Sometimes you will be given more information, sometimes less, in every case you will be given the exact right amount of information to accomplish what God wants to accomplish both in the situation he sends you to and in your own hearts."

He seemed really to emphasize that part of our own hearts, and he was looking right at me as he said it.

But, that really wasn't helping us much, so I brushed it off, and we got down to business.

For those of you who know anything about us, business always starts the exact same way. And so it was we all knelt to pray, and one by one poured our hearts out to the God who loves us and thinks enough of us to use us when we are not worthy of being used.

Chapter Four

By the time we were done praying, we looked up, and the Conductor was gone, and we knew it was no use trying to find him.

"Well," Aly said, "there is no present like time and no time like the present."

"That, Squirt, is truly profound. Let's go."

With that, we started down the mountain heading in the general direction of the valley below. The sun had risen just barely, and the lovely evergreen boughs overhead were filtering the light down to us in such a way that it seemed the very sunlight of heaven was illuminating our pathway.

For some reason, I turned to look back toward the cave that we had left a few hundred yards behind us. When I did, I noticed smoke rising through a fissure in the rock, and drifting oh, so high into the sky.

"Guys, we're forgetting mom and dad's rule. Someone didn't turn the light off before we left," I said as I pointed back toward the cave.

"I got this, bro," Aly said. Immediately there were pine needles and dirt flying out from under her feet as she raced back up the path. In three or four minutes, the torch had been extinguished, she was back with us, and we were once again headed down the mountain.

Periodically the green and brown gave way to a bright splash of orange. Those who have been in the Georgia or North Carolina mountains know that every now and then an orange mountain azalea will spring up. There really is no color quite like that one.

We walked on in silence for a good while, at least as silent as things get in the forest. With the babbling of the occasional brook, the birds chirping, the wind whistling, and the occasional unidentified beast snorting or growling, silence is actually somewhat of a relative term.

After about an hour, the terrain flattened out, and we broke out of the woods into an open valley. There up ahead of us was the town the conductor had told us of, containing whatever unidentified trouble there was that we were there to deal with. Instinctively we stopped, gathered close together, and just watched for a little while. It was always better to see before being seen.

"What do you think, Carrie?"

"Well, your eyes are better than mine, but it certainly looks like a very peaceful, placid place, at least from this distance."

"Maybe," Aly said, "but what say we be careful anyway. I didn't exactly come prepared for this."

None of us had. We did not have the night packs we usually curled up with just in case, no pocket knives, no nothing. We absolutely had not even considered the possibility that we might be called into an adventure during the week of camp.

We started off down the trail heading toward the town. It looked like it would take us maybe three or four minutes to get there, so along the way Carrie filled us in just a little bit with what she remembered about the area from her history studies.

"A man named Captain Juan Pardo passed through Towns County in 1567. He was looking for gold. Several of the towns his journal mentions correspond to Creek Indian town names in northeast Georgia. He probably followed the same route as the French. Something clearly went wrong along the way, and reports eventually reached the Spanish capital at Santa Elena that all of the forts in the mountains had been massacred. This area was known for its violence but was also somewhat shrouded in mystery."

"Duly noted, Sis," I said with determination, "we will be careful and watchful."

A few moments of walking quickly passed and all too soon our feet touched the hard packed dirt of the little town. As with many of the old towns we have been in, there wasn't much to it. Maybe twenty buildings at most, and not more than a handful of them of any substantial size. As expected, there was some type of an inn/saloon structure near the center of town. Surprisingly, though, there did not seem to be a church anywhere. That we definitely were not used to, and that put us all the more on guard.

"No church," Aly said with disapproval. "That's never a good sign."

I just nodded, and we made our way into the town center. We turned left just a bit to make our way up toward the inn, but suddenly Carrie put both of her arms out and stopped us all dead in our tracks.

"What gives, genius girl?"

"The nothingness," she answered. Seeing the perplexed looks on my face and on Aly's, she continued with a further explanation. "When is the last time we ever went into an old town that was this dead quiet?"

She was right. The three of us got so quiet that even our breathing didn't make noise. But despite our own silence, we couldn't hear anything else either. No music, no talking, no laughing, no chewing, nothing. It was as if everyone was holding their breath.

"Let's go in," I whispered, "and see what's up."

The echoing of our footsteps on the wooden stairs and slat board gangplank sounded like cannon fire against the backdrop of the utter silence. I really felt like stopping, turning around, and bolting back out of town. None of this felt right. But dad says that sometimes you just have to pin your ears back and bull ahead, so I did. With Carrie and Aly right on my heels, I pushed through the swinging batwing doors and walked straight into the obvious source of silence.

There were at least twenty white people in the room, all of them holding their breath and staring intently at the one white person who had gone beyond white and become utterly pale. I guess that is pretty easy to happen when a really large Indian has an incredibly mean looking blade held hard against your throat and so much anger and hatred in his eyes that you knew at any moment he was going to flick his wrist and end your life.

As we three Night Heroes came to a halt just inside the room, the big Indian never even turned his head our way. He did, though, apparently have excellent peripheral vision.

"Welcome, children of the white man. Today you will see one of your own die."

If this is what we had been sent for, we were automatically at a distinct disadvantage. There was no offensive action we could take that would save the man's life whose neck was quivering against the cold steel of the Indian's blade. I was utterly unsure what to do. Carrie, though, not so much.

"No, great warrior, I do not believe that we shall. The Great Spirit sent us here for a reason. And I do not believe for a moment that reason was to watch a man die."

"And what do children of the white man know of the Great Spirit?" The big Indian asked contemptuously.

"More than you may realize," Carrie answered pleasantly. "He has revealed Himself to us in our sacred writings and in His dealings in our lives. He directs our paths and shows us things that we did not know."

"You know nothing of the Great Spirit," he spat. "And He has revealed nothing to you. You speak lies, as do all white men."

This was going bad in a hurry. I hoped Carrie knew what she was doing.

"Do I? Tell me, great warrior, when shall the serpent arise from the ashes, and whom shall he bite when he does?"

Man oh man, what a change came over that big Indian! His eyes got wide, his face got pale, and his hand began to shake. And then suddenly, quicker than I've ever seen a man move, he jerked back his hand, punched the man in the jaw, and launched his body through the glass window and out the back of the inn.

Screaming like a wild banshee, he disappeared up into the hills.

Chapter Five

The noise of a couple of dozen people all letting out their breath at once is louder than you might imagine. Once everyone had exhaled then replenished their breath, people began to rush over to their fallen friend. The loud "crack" as the Indian hit him in the jaw told me he would likely be out cold for a good while.

"That blasted Indian needs to die," spat a wizened old man with a skewed hat and long white whiskers.

That comment brought immediate agreement, shouts of approval, and roars of red hatred from the motley assembly in the room. I did not know what was going on, but I did know that this crowd would very likely track that Indian down and have him dead by nightfall.

"Wait, my brothers, wait," came a calm voice from the shadows.

I turned slightly and saw a man with a dark tan kind of like my dad's step into the center of the room. He was a tall man, thin and wiry, but he seemed to be very strong. He also seemed fluid, almost graceful, in his movements, although to be honest, his head looked sort of, well, deformed and pointy in the back. There was a calm, reassuring quality to his voice, and a rhythm and timing to it much like a metronome.

"I know you are all angry, and rightly so. Rain Water has cause trouble here yet again. But it is not just him; he is merely the tip of the spear, so to speak. Your crops are stolen, and your families starve because of his tribe, not just him. Your women and daughters disappear because of the lust of his warriors, not just him. The peace of your town is shattered over and over because of the raining arrows of his tribe, not just him. Dealing with him alone will merely open the door for another to take his place. Yes, he must be dealt with, but not by himself."

All of the men in the room were silently nodding their heads in agreement. And when I say all, I mean myself as well. It was Carrie's sharp voice that snapped me out of my near hypnotic state.

"Pardon me, are you suggesting that an entire tribe be wiped out?"

The man whirled like a flash, and for the briefest of moments I thought I saw a flash of violent anger on his face. But I must have been wrong because the kind smile and soft eyes of this man told me he was not one given to anger.

"Young lady, I do not know who you are, or where you are from, but if you had been here long enough to hear the wailing of mothers who had their babies ripped from their arms, if you had been here long enough to see the broken hearts of young widows whose husbands had been slaughtered and scalped in front of their eyes, then you would have more pity for our dilemma. We have tried everything imaginable to make peace with Rain Water and his particular band of the Creeks, but they want none of it. If something is not done, and soon, all of us will be dead. Given those circumstances, what would you have us to do?"

Carrie had nothing to say. That, friends, is a rare thing.

The tall man smiled kindly at us and then turned away to discuss further plans with the men in that room. It was clear that we had been dismissed, and dismissed like school children who have been lovingly lectured by a busy principle.

We Night Heroes, not feeling so heroic at the moment, turned and walked out the way we came. My emotional state could best be described as confused anger. It was clear to me that the big Indian was a problem that needed to be dealt with, I just wasn't sure of all the details yet. Aly, for her part, was...chasing a butterfly. That's my littlest sister: nearly caught up in a life-threatening brawl one moment, happily chasing a butterfly the next. I wasn't worried about her, though. She is as happy-go-lucky as the day is long. But when the action finally starts in earnest, she is pure lightning in a bottle.

Carrie seemed confused. That wasn't at all like her, figuring things out was as easy as breathing to her.

"What do you think, Sis?"

"I don't know, Kyle, I really don't know."

"Well," I said, "clearly, at least for the moment, our mission is not in that room. We still have several hours of daylight left before we go to sleep for our trip back to our day, so, it seems like the logical thing to do would be to track Rain Water as far as we can and see where that leads us and what we can learn."

"Yeah, I suppose so," Carrie said softly.

"Are you going to be okay, Sis?"

"Sure, I'll be fine. I just need to work some things out in my head. What about you?"

"I'm fine," I said. "Let's just get to it and see if we can track that big Indian."

I smiled as I said it. But as Carrie called to Aly to come with us, I mumbled under my breath, "I have seen your kind before, Indian, and I will deal with you as I dealt with him."

We spent the next several hours hiking up the mountains and through the passes of North Georgia. This big Indian had a long stride, and he was very good in the woods. He left very little sign of his passing, nothing more than a pebble kicked out of its indentation in the ground, or a tiny broken twig, or a smudged spot in the soft dirt as he rounded a tree. Fortunately, we had in our previous adventure in the mountains of Rogersville become better than average at reading those tiny, telltale signs.

About an hour before dusk, we began to hear some soft chanting in the trees further up the side of the mountain. We instinctively stopped, crouched, and began to slowly and softly crawl the rest of the way. It took us maybe a half hour, but we were finally able to peer just over the top of the ridge and see a cozy little campsite nestled amongst the rocks, in a clearing on the top of the mountain.

There, in that campsite, were two or three young braves, a couple of Indian ladies, a few children, and in the center of it all, kneeling, with his hands spread toward heaven, Rain Water.

We watched silently for a few minutes. Then, knowing our time was short, we moved back down the hillside without the faintest trace of any noise. We made our way maybe a quarter mile further down and found the recent deadfall of a tree right beside a noisy little brook. We crawled under the tree to settle down for our final few minutes of the first day/night of our newest adventure. We then began to talk, softly, though we knew that the tree boughs and the sound of the brook would completely drown out the sound of our voices.

"Well, that was productive, I think. We now know what those men down in town do not; the location of Rain Water's campsite. He doubtless has far more people in his tribe scattered throughout these hills somewhere, but this seems to be the folks that are nearest to him."

"And what are you planning on doing with that information, Kyle?" Carrie asked somewhat accusingly.

I sort of knew she would ask, and that she would ask that way.

"Carrie, let's not fight, we are on the same team." And then, partially because I wanted to know and partially to change the subject, I asked, "By the way, how did you know to bring up that snake rising from the ashes? How did you know it would save that man's life by getting Rain Water to run? What part of your history expertise let you know all that?"

She smiled. "History? None. I still don't have any idea what it means. I was actually relying more on theology that history."

"Um, theology?" Aly asked with a face twisted up in confusion.

"Yeah, theology. The fact that God does everything He does for a reason and makes no mistakes. There has to be a reason He had our arrival point in this adventure be that cave with that drawing. It has to somehow be significant. Beyond that, I was just spitballing, hoping something I said would stick."

"Wow, spitball theology," Aly said as she rolled her eyes and shook her head. We all laughed at that, then leaned back on the trunk of the tree, closed our eyes, and let the lovely song of the brook sing us to sleep.

Chapter Six

If you have read any of our previous adventures, you are probably expecting at this point to read something like, *"We awoke to the low humming of the air conditioner in the hotel room..."*

But the cabins at Camp Hosanna are not air conditioned. And "awoke" is not quite the right word for being jolted to consciousness by some of the camp counselors shouting at the top of their lungs, "We kickin, we kickin, hit em in the head with a big fat chicken! We awesome, we awesome, hit em in the head with a big fat possum!"

Instinctively, I rolled up onto one knee in a defensive posture and looked around for Carrie and Aly. It only took a split second for me to realize when and where I was and that my sisters were in another cabin with a bunch of other girls. We would not be waking up together each day to discuss the adventures of the night before.

Seeing what he surely had to regard as my "odd behavior," Zach raised an eyebrow at me and said, "Easy, breezy, it's all good. No monsters here."

From there we were up, dressed, and quickly got busy cleaning the cabin. This was important, nearly off-the-charts essential; it would determine what order we got to eat meals in. Get the cleanest cabin, go first. The worse your cabin, the farther back in the line you all had to go.

After a few minutes of cleaning, we were out the door pretty quickly. The chuckwagon bell was chiming, and none of us wanted to be the last one there.

The sweet ladies at camp had, of course, gone all out for our breakfast. There was French Toast, eggs, grits, juice, and cake. Yes, cake. Go figure! We scarfed all of that down, laughing, talking, and cutting up the entire time.

When breakfast was done, we rushed back to the cabin to clean for a few more minutes and to leave some gifts (otherwise known as bribes; chocolate, candy, that kind of thing) for those who would be judging the cabins. Hey, this was war, and we intended to win!

Maybe twenty minutes later, we all headed back to the meeting hall. Dad was set up to preach. We already knew that he would be doing a series on the life of Samson during the morning sessions. He always calls that series "Like Any Other Man," which is an exact phrase taken from Samson's own mouth recorded in Judges 16:17. Samson had his head resting in wicked Delilah's lap as he said those words. How incredibly foolish to regard an enemy of God as someone you can trust! That mistake cost Samson everything.

Dad's first message on that was "You have YOU trouble." Most people think that Samson had woman trouble. After all, Delilah was not even the first Philistine girl he went chasing. His mom and dad, in frustration, actually asked him, "Is there NEVER a woman among the daughters of thy brethren, or among all my people, that thou goest to take a wife of the uncircumcised Philistines?" Samson, bless his carnal heart, answered back, "Get her for me; for she pleaseth me well." That guy wanted what he wanted, when he wanted it, and no one could ever talk him out of it. No wonder he got into so much trouble! A guy or girl that ignores the godly counsel of mom and dad and pastor and won't obey the Bible is headed for disaster as fast as he can go.

Anyway, I watched the rest of the kids as dad preached, and they all listened really well. That told me that they all probably had good pastors who had taught them how

47

important it is to listen while God's man is preaching.

I tried to listen well also. But I have to admit, I was probably more distracted than most. Not by thoughts of a big Indian terrorizing a village, an adventure we would have to deal with without ever saying anything to anyone, but by another big problem.

Drew.

Still wearing that long sleeve leather jacket.

He was watching dad, and he was doing so far more closely than anyone else. I immediately tensed up; if he did anything wrong, if he lunged at dad, it was on. I knew Dad could handle himself; I have seen him in action. A German soldier found that out the hard way. That is another story, a long one, from our second adventure. Anyway, I knew Dad could handle himself, but I had already made up my mind that he wouldn't have to.

I shook my head to clear the cobwebs, just in time to hear Dad ask everyone to stand. I have no idea how long I was "out of it" daydreaming about trouble from Drew. What had I missed during the message? Rats, I hate it when I let my mind wander like that, preaching is too important, too precious to ignore.

The invitation was given, and a goodly number of young people came to the altar to pray about their walk with the Lord.

Drew didn't come. I didn't either. I told myself it was because I was being protective of my dad, but something (or Someone) in my heart was telling me different.

Mom and dad disappeared after service. I figured they had headed into town for supplies, but with them, it is also possible they headed off on a hike up into the mountains. They really seem to like being alone together.

"Hey, bro, whatcha think?"

I snapped back to attention and saw Aly beside me. "I think he is trouble with a capital T, and will need to be dealt with, most likely harshly."

"What about the women and children? They seem to be dependent on him, and they didn't seem to be at all war-like."

"What? Women and children? What are you talking about, the kitchen ladies? The girls in your cabin? What do they have to do with him?"

Aly scrunched up her forehead and squinted at me, looking half way confused and the other half miffed.

"Huh? Are you talking about Drew again? I was talking about Rain Water. What in the world has gotten into you?"

I didn't have time to answer, and I was glad. Brother Abbott had blown the whistle and was using the megaphone to summon all of us to the middle of the field. I whirled away from Aly and raced out there and got more excited with each step I took.

Hillbilly Basketball, a Camp Hosanna original! Some of the counselors had already described it to me, and I was amped up over it.

In the center of the field was a very tall pole, and fastened at the top were a few square plastic crates with the bottoms cut out. There were some kick balls laying around, as well as a bunch of swimming pool noodles that had been cut in half.

Brother Abbott explained the game to all of us. The girls would always be on defense, and they would have the pool noodles to beat us with. The girls from one team would guard/assault the guys from the other team. There would be several rounds with a set amount of time, and the team that got the most goals in that time would win.

Pool. Noodles. Hurt. Especially when they are being swung by Olivia Abbott, Brother Abbott's oldest daughter. She can play the guitar, she can sing, she clearly loves the Lord, but none of those good qualities kept her from nearly knocking my head into the next dimension!

I have been in a fight with rough and tumble miners in the coal war of 1912. I have tumbled over an embankment while fighting with a Union Soldier during the battle of Chickamauga. I think I would do either of those things again rather than go through ten more minutes of teenage girls unleashing all of the frustrations of their entire lives out on me by whacking me over the head and in the face with pool noodles.

But, we did win, so I guess all's well that ends well.

Drew didn't play.

Biggest guy in camp, and he sat off to the side in that black leather jacket, staring straight ahead with a stone face.

Lunch was every bit as good as breakfast. Then things got even better! The counselors rushed us to the cabins, we got into some clothes we could get wet, and we rushed back down to the creek. Everyone grabbed an inner tube, and we headed up to the head of the creek. That began a couple of glorious hours of riding down the creek, getting out, rushing back to the starting point, and then doing it all over again.

That had to be some of the coldest water I have ever felt. But after getting hot and sweaty in the fields games, it was simply amazing.

Once our tubing time was over, we headed out to the field and played football until we were good and dry. Then it was over to the bathhouses for our showers, and before we knew it, the dinner bell was clanging once again.

Hot dogs and hamburgers. Glooooorious! If I said I ate two of each I would be short selling it by one. Yes, three hotdogs and three hamburgers, and no regrets. Dad often says, "If I ate like you, I would have a heart attack within a week." But he is always smiling as he says it. I suspect he used to eat just like me when he was a kid.

When supper was over, we went back to the cabins for some personal devotion time, and then when the meeting hall was reset, we all came back down for service. I caught sight of Carrie and Aly as they walked across the field. I had to admit, my sisters are very pretty. Mind you, I would never tell them that. But the best part about them was the inside–they both love the Lord and walk close to Him. Any brother would be proud to have them as sisters.

The night service was better than good; it was amazing. Dad preached a message you may have heard me mention before in other books, *Choosing Your Final Destination.* It examines in detail what heaven and hell are really like. For the life of me, I cannot understand why anybody with a rational mind would choose to reject Christ and go to that awful place called hell. Especially when such an amazing place as heaven is available to us instead!

Thankfully, eight young people decided that they felt the same way about it, and came to the altar and asked Jesus to forgive them of their sins and come into their heart. It simply doesn't get any better than seeing a bunch of people born again!

After the service, we broke up into smaller groups and went out into the field to pray and have some devotion time for a little while. Then it was back to the cabins for a night of uninterrupted sleep. For everyone but my sisters and I, that is. For us, as soon as we fell asleep it would be time to get down to business.

Chapter Seven

I awoke to the muted mumblings of Carrie and Aly talking to the Conductor. As I rolled over and took stock of my surroundings, I realized we were waking up in the cave for the second day. The light was just beginning to shine into the entrance, and Carrie and Aly, who like me had come much more prepared this time, were shining their flashlights on the drawings on the wall.

"No sir," Carrie said to the conductor as she shook her head from side to side, "I'm still not certain what they mean. Being as how we are at camp all day during the day, I haven't had the opportunity to get out and do any research. That could end up being a severe hindrance to us."

"And do you think that caught the Lord by surprise?" He asked with a smile.

Carrie smiled back and with genuine pleasantness said, "Certainly not, not at all. All of us Night Heroes know that nothing ever catches God off guard."

"Good." He responded firmly. "In that case, you will just have to trust Him to provide you with the information you need from an unlikely source since your normal likely sources are currently unavailable to you."

I got up and stretched, a huge, bone cracking kind of stretch, one that felt like a million bucks.

"So, what do we know, and what do we have? It seems to me that just like back in Rogersville, we have an Indian problem."

"It seems to me," Aly said with just the slightest hint of a strain in her voice, "that you have forgotten Proverbs 18:13."

I hated to admit it right then, but the squirt was right. I had forgotten what that verse said. But I had the strangest hunch she was about to tell me. That hunch proved immediately to be correct.

"He that answereth a matter before he heareth it, it is folly and shame unto him."

"I have heard it, Aly," I said. "I heard it yesterday when that man in the inn told us all that Rain Water has done."

"In that case, you have heard exactly one side of the story."

"Aly, you're just going to have to trust me on this one. I know a bad apple when I see one."

Carrie and Aly just looked at me, and then looked over the Conductor. He had a very blank, unreadable look on his face; I saw neither approval or disapproval in it. If he had been a poker player at that moment, I would have given him a good chance of winning no matter what hand he was holding.

After a moment of silence, he said, "I will leave you three to your work now. What you do is up to you, but I will say this, you seem to be leaning very much on the past to help you make your present decisions. But sometimes the past is not at all what it seems, and therefore, the course that it lays in the present may not be straight and true."

With those cryptic words, the conductor walked out in the sunlight. As our eyes momentarily closed and watered as we turned toward that light, I knew that when we opened them, he would be gone.

"Well, Senior Night Hero, what is our plan of attack for the day?" Carrie asked without much enthusiasm in her voice.

"I've been thinking about that," I said. "Problem-solving 101. What is the problem, at least as far as we know, and what is the solution?"

"Well," my big brained sister began, "if we take the facts only as far as the known facts themselves allow, the fact that we walked into a situation yesterday in which a man had a knife held to his throat by an Indian, and the fact that after the Indian left, people begin to speak of killing his entire tribe, those two things tell us that there's a conflict between the white man and the Indians in this area.

"What those two facts do not necessarily tell us is how the conflict started, or who is primarily responsible." As she said that, she said it slowly and deliberately and looked me eyeball to eyeball as she did. I knew what she was getting at, and I was prepared for it. Since both of my sisters needed some convincing to come around to the right way of thinking, I would be gracious and go along with them. Dad always says a little graciousness goes a long way, and that it is easier to catch flies with honey than with vinegar.

"Duly noted, sis. That being the case, here is my proposal for the day. That tall man with the odd shaped head spoke of all of the people that have been harmed by Rain Water and his tribe. Why don't we make our way back into town and see if we can actually speak to some people about what has gone on? They may well be able to either confirm or deny the accusations being made."

Carrie got a rather impressed look on her face, and said, "Hmm. That's not at all what I expected to hear. But I have to admit it makes perfect sense, so let's go with it."

I nodded and took the lead heading out of the cave. Aly fell in behind me, and Carrie fell in behind her. If they had been out front and able to see my face, I suspect they would've seen a bit of a smirk. I was getting my sisters to do exactly what I needed them to do; I was getting them to go ask the victims of Rain Water's violence what had happened. When they heard all that these poor people would surely say, it would bring them around to my point of view, and we could get down to business. Yes, I hate to waste time like that, but I had enough sense to know that my sisters and I are better as a team, and therefore we needed to get our act together and get unified on this.

The morning's walk was every bit as lovely as the day before. How in the world anyone could take a look at nature and not see nature's God behind it was just beyond me. Life simply does not come from nonliving material, especially not life as varied and marvelous as the teeming magnificent life on earth. Plant life, animal life, birds and insects, microbes, bacteria, so much life is clearly a testimony to a living God, and I am glad that I know Him personally.

It took about the same amount of time as yesterday to reach the outskirts of town. Realizing that we had forgotten to pray, we stopped and did so. We poured our hearts out to God asking Him for safety, but also asking Him for wisdom. Proverbs 1 tells us that even a young person has wisdom available to him, and we clearly needed it.

After we had said "Amen," we made our way side-by-side, one tall bull-strong teenage boy, one genius and godly teenage girl, and one slightly preteen firecracker, into the town. The first people we saw were two ladies carrying baskets of something or other toward a nondescript building just up ahead and to the right of us. We swerved slightly in their direction and intercepted them up on the porch.

"Pardon me, ladies," I said pleasantly, "may we have a moment of your time?"

The two ladies looked at each other, seeming a bit nervous, but then sat down on a bench and agreed to speak to us.

"What can we do for you fine young people today?" the older of the two asked.

"Well, ma'am, we were in town yesterday for all of the, um, action at the inn. We don't want to get ourselves in any trouble while we are here since we are just passing through, so we thought we would ask some folks what exactly is going on. The more we know, the more we can watch our step."

The ladies looked at each other once again as if they were speaking to each other with their eyes, and trying to make a decision. After a couple of tense, silent seconds, the younger of the two turned back toward us and spoke.

"They took my husband," she said as her voice began to quiver just a bit. "We had only been married for a month, and those savages took him. It was eleven months ago. I have searched the hills and hollows myself, the men from the town have searched, and there has been nary a sight of him. He kissed me goodbye that morning, went to do his work in the field, and never returned."

As she said that, the dam broke. She began to sob and wail uncontrollably as the older of the two ladies wrapped her arms around her, pulled her to her chest, stroked her hair, and begin to coo soft words of comfort to her. As she did, the older lady looked up at us, and the look on her face sent an unmistakable message: you have opened a wound, and you need to leave now.

We thanked them for their help and walked off of the porch and farther on into the town. Just across the street a building or two up there was an old man sitting and whittling. We walked up onto the porch and greeted him, and as we did he spat some tobacco juice out of his mouth (nasty!) and told us to "set a spell." We thankfully obliged him.

"Sir," I said, "could you possibly tell us what's going on around here? What exactly is happening between Rain Water and his tribe and the town folks?"

The old man spat again this time out of anger, not out of an excess of nasty brown juice trapped in his mouth.

"Ain't you got eyes, boy? We got Indian trouble; I got Indian trouble."

Aly looked up at him, and I recognized the look on her face. It was her puppy dog eyes. That is the exact same look she always uses when she wants to wrap my dad around her finger and wheedle something out of him.

"What kind of Indian trouble? What did that awful Indian do to you?"

The old man looked at her as if he was looking at his own precious granddaughter. I knew that was exactly the effect she had intended, and that this man was about to spill his guts.

"Well, sweetheart, I don't want to scare you, but that Indian is heap bad medicine, as they say. Why do you think I'm sitting on this porch whittling instead of doing something productive? Not quite a year ago, I had some great corn crops growing, I was about to have a huge harvest, enough to pay off my land entirely. And then one morning I woke to the smell of smoke! I jumped out of bed and rushed out the door in time to see my entire corn crop going up in flames. That blasted Indian burned my fields down, and I lost pert near everything. Had to sell my land and move to a little room here in town."

"Thank you, sir," I said, "we sure do appreciate your time."

We left the old man sitting on the porch, whittling and spitting and spitting and whittling. Our next stop was the inn, the scene of yesterday's near fatality.

As we walk in, we noticed that it was remarkably less crowded and more peaceful than the day before. I figured everyone was afraid Rain Water may come back and catch them by surprise. There was the man behind the counter washing glasses and a small handful of people scattered at different tables.

We sized up the room and the people and made our way over to a table in the corner where a bald, studious looking little man was sitting.

"Pardon me, sir," I said with a pleasant smile, "May we have a moment of your time?"

He motioned for us to sit, and we took him up on his offer.

"If you don't mind me asking, what exactly is going on around here between Rain Water and his tribe and the townsfolk?"

The man dropped his head a bit and shook it sadly from side to side. "That Indian has ruined my life," he said. "I am, or rather was, the town banker. That all changed the morning that I came into work and found that the bank had been broken into during the night. Every bit of money or gold within it had been stolen. The only reason the people in town haven't killed me is because they are so anxious to kill the big Indian that took their money from me."

"How long ago was that?" Carrie asked.

"Just two months ago," he responded sadly. "I do not know how I shall ever recover; I shall likely have to move back to Virginia."

The rest of the day went just like that. A lady came home from shopping in town to find her dead husband lying scalped in the front yard four months ago. Another lady just three months ago had her children go missing during the night. A young husband seven months ago heard his wife scream from the garden out back and by the time he got out there she had vanished without a trace.

Daylight was fading fast, and we had heard enough. As far as I was concerned, we should use the rest of our time to track Rain Water again and see if he was still in the same camp. Carrie though was insistent that we go back to the cave for our nightly trip back to our time. I was gracious enough to oblige her;

mostly because I knew that I would still have time over the next three days to track Rain Water down and deal with him.

We got back to the cave just as it was getting dark. Carrie went right back to the drawings and began to study them furiously. She was mumbling to herself like a girl possessed and seemed to be desperate to figure something or other out. No matter which side of the wall she went to she always came back to the very center picture that of the serpent rising out of the blue pile of ashes.

She touched it with her finger and then looked at her finger. It was blue, the dye or chalk or whatever it was had gotten onto it. But though she seemed fascinated by that, to me it was time to press the more important issue.

"Well, sis," I said, "did talking to all those people in town today help clear things up for you?"

"As a matter of fact it did, Kyle," she said. "Tell me, what did every single account have in common?"

That question threw me just a little bit. I stammered, "Well, uh,"

"Think, Kyle, think. You are so used to fighting that you have forgotten how to use your brain," she said angrily.

That got me hot in a hurry, friend, so I snapped right back at her.

"Spit it out, sis, show off that genius intellect of yours one more time. What exactly did all of those accounts that we heard today have in common? Tell me, oh great one, enlighten your ignorant brother."

"Fine." She said. "All of those accounts, one tragedy after another, all of them had exactly one thing in common: no one at any time saw an Indian."

Chapter Eight

I suppose my breakfast would have been good if it didn't taste quite so much like crow. I knew that I was still right and that Rain Water was behind everything, but I also knew that Carrie had a valid point, one that I should have noticed. I had gone to sleep thinking about it and woke right back up at camp still thinking about it.

As I poked at my grits with my spoon, Brother Abbott walked over and sat down beside me. "What's up, young man," he asked, "you seem sort of distracted this morning."

"Ahh, nothing really, I suppose."

"In my experience, 'nothing really' usually means 'quite a bit.'"

I smiled just a little bit, and said, "That's pretty perceptive. I guess I'm just having some disagreements with some people that I am close to, and I am having trouble getting them to see things my way."

"Oh, is that all?" He asked cheerfully. "In that case, I can absolutely help you."

That really caught my attention, so I turned to face him straight on and said, "Really? How?"

"Well, the best way to fix people not seeing things your way is for you to start seeing things God's way. That way, when they start seeing things God's way, they'll also be seeing them your way. And if they don't start seeing things your way, at least you are still seeing things God's way."

It took me a few seconds to process all of that, as it sounded remarkably like something my dad would say; intentionally confusing yet completely accurate. In other words, designed to make a person think.

"I think I see your point. But how do I know that I'm not already seeing things God's way on the issue I am facing?"

"Well, you could start with the fact that you look like you swallowed a live possum who had just eaten a half pound of persimmons. Most people that see things God's way have this thing that the Bible calls, 'the peace that passes all understanding.' You have about as much peace on your face as I do hair on my head."

I couldn't help but laugh at that since Brother Abbott doesn't have much hair anymore.

Brother Abbott got up and went on about his way, and I went with my cabin mates back to the cabin to clean. A few minutes later we were back down there, and the morning service was beginning.

Dad preached his second part of the Samson series, "A Miracle with Only a Temporary Effect." Samson got trapped in Gaza, thirty-five miles southwest of home, in the far southern tip of Philistine territory. Some men were laying wait outside the city to kill him. At midnight, he got up, yanked up the city gates that weighed thousands of pounds and carried them twenty miles away.

But the very next thing we read is Judges 16:4, which says, "And it came to pass afterward, that he loved a woman in the valley of Sorek, whose name was Delilah." God gave Sampson a miracle, yet Samson went right back to his sinful ways.

I guess it's like my dad always says, if Christ dying on Calvary for you isn't enough to make a child of God live right, nothing else will be either.

Once the service was done, mom and dad disappeared again. I think they were going down to Helen, Georgia, to eat some German food.

We guys went out onto the field to play swimming pool kickball. Each base was either a bucket or tub or kiddie pool full of ice-cold water. That made for an incredibly wet, sloppy, sloshy game. In other words, we all loved it.

As for me, I was laughing and cutting up and running and putting everything into it, I was thoroughly enjoying myself until I saw Carrie over by the volleyball courts...

Talking to Drew.

Hi, this is Carrie, I will pick up the story from here for now.

The guys had been busy playing swimming pool kickball. We girls had been playing flag football, but I had to come out of the game for a few minutes to let another girl in. I wandered about thirty feet away, and as I did my mind wandered with me. Each step took my thoughts farther back in time, back, back, back, to the year 1780 and a riddle wrapped in an enigma.

Standing there thinking, I held up my hand and stared at my index finger. I knew that the key to our riddle was somehow tied in with that cave drawing of the serpent rising out of the blue ashes. My finger was still just as blue as it had been the night before, more than two hundred years ago. Odd, that.

"It's Maya blue," a voice behind me said.

Snapping back to the present, I whirled around to see who was speaking to me. It was Drew, and he was looking at my finger as if it were the oddest thing in the world.

"What?" I said.

"The color on your finger. It's Maya blue."

I just looked at him, utterly confused about both him and the color on my finger and why he was calling it what he was calling it.

"Sorry, I'm being weird. At least until I explain myself, I guess. I have Tetrachromacy. Most people have the standard three types of cone shaped cells in their eyes that allows them to see about 1 million different colors. People like me with Tetrachromacy have a fourth type of cone shaped cell in their eye to go along with the other three. We can see the subtle variations in colors that others cannot see. My eye can make out nearly 100 million different colors, and once I have seen a color I never forget it.

"That color on your finger, though, is extra unforgettable. The only place it can be found in the entire world is in the Mayan ruins of Mexico. My family and I visited there once.

The Mayans used it in their worship services and in their sacrifices. It is made by combining Indigo Dye from the leaves of a certain plant with a clay called palygorskite.

"So, I'm just curious, how does a girl from North Carolina who is currently at a Christian camp in Georgia have a color on her finger that can only be found in the Mayan ruins of Mexico?"

As he said that, there was no trace of anything sinister in his voice, just a genuine curiosity that for the moment seemed to have pulled him out of his shell. I could tell that he really wanted to know about that color. He had no idea how much I wanted to know about it as well; nor did he know how much information he had already given me, and how much that extra information had complicated an already tangled riddle in my mind.

I knew I needed to answer him somehow, and quickly.

"Well," I said, "I have certainly never been to Mexico, Mayan ruins or otherwise. So I guess that makes this color on my finger a mystery to both of us! Thank you for the information, though, it is fascinating, and I definitely want to do some studying on it."

And then something hit me, something else that needed to be said.

"Does anyone else know how brilliant you are? You seem to be going out of your way to hide it, but everything you just said tells me that you have a way-above-average intellect to go along with your way-above-average color perception."

He turned really, really red at that moment, and I instantly felt bad. It had not been my intention to embarrass him.

"No, I guess not," he said. "It isn't really something that I talk about; people think I'm weird enough anyway."

"I don't think you're weird, Drew, not any weirder than any of the rest of us. We all have our issues that we have to deal with and work through. We also all have a God who loves us dearly and wants us to be saved, so that we can spend eternity in heaven with Him."

He just shook his head "yes" a little bit at that, and then turned and walked away. I clearly had given him some things to think about.

But little did he know, he had given me far more to think about.

Chapter Nine

Hey, this is Kyle again. I had watched Carrie and Drew have their conversation and had grown angrier by the minute. At least at first. But then Brother Abbott's words to me from just a little bit ago came ringing back into my heart and my head. Me being angry about my sister talking to Drew, knowing how godly she was and how wise, was most certainly not the kind of thoughts that Christ would be thinking.

I also knew that she could handle herself in pretty much any situation, so even once I put my anger aside, it would be foolish for me to replace it with something like worry.

I went back to concentrating on our game and actually seemed to have more of a peaceful and light heart. The rest of the afternoon was filled with games, Brother Abbott and his staff made sure that every day was jam packed with things we would never forget.

Late in the afternoon, we once again showered off and got cleaned up for supper. It was an amazingly good spaghetti and salad supper. When we were done, we went out back and played a few minutes of basketball, and then helped to reset the meetinghouse for the night service.

Dad preached on "The Mark of the Beast." That is always a sobering and somewhat frightening message, mostly because it is all true and will probably happen very soon. The Bible describes a wicked man known as Antichrist and the Mark of the Beast that he will require people to take during the tribulation period. I am just glad that as a Christian, I will not have to be there for that.

Two more young ladies were saved that night. There were tears and smiles all around as we rejoiced over God birthing two more precious souls into His family

Once the service was done, we once again went out by cabins into the field and spent some time testifying and doing some devotions. We sang some songs and worshiped the God who made us and is so very good to us.

Normally, we would have gone right from there to the cabins to get some sleep. But on that night, Brother Abbott and Brother Wood and the staff had something special whipped up for us, an amazing fireworks display. Man, let me tell you: there is no sound quite so amazing as the sound of high-powered fireworks exploding and then echoing off of the mountains surrounding the camp and coming right back to you. It is like sound waves crashing into other sound waves and then crashing into your ear.

We oohed and ahhed over all of the colors and noises, we cheered every time an especially large firework went off, we high-fived and clapped, and in general just had the time of our lives.

But finally the fireworks came to an end, and it was once again time for everyone else to go to sleep and stay there, and my sisters and I to go to sleep and get to work.

The cabins at Camp Hosanna

The playing field and meeting house

Girls Basketball

Gavin doing his best impersonation of Brother Abbott.

One of the "Bacon Girls"

Chapter Ten

Is a very disconcerting thing to wake up and realize that someone is sitting nearby staring at you. But there she was, my sister Carrie, sitting cross-legged about three feet away from me and staring at me. I could hear Aly singing a happy, chirpy song from somewhere just outside the cave. The Conductor was nowhere to be seen, I was guessing that for whatever reason we were on our own for the day.

"Something isn't right, Kyle."

"I agree, sis, you are creeping me out by staring at me, and that definitely isn't right."

"I'm serious, Kyle, something isn't right about all of this, and if we don't figure it out, we are going to make a huge mistake."

I could hear an urgency in her voice, a pleading. That was not like her, she was really concerned.

I rolled over and sat up and said, "Talk to me. What's going on?"

She began to explain to me what she had learned about the blue ashes on the wall that the serpent was rising out of.

"Tetrachromacy? Maya blue? Sis, all of that seems kind of far-fetched and unbelievable.

"What, you mean like three kids going to sleep at night and waking up hundreds of years in the past?"

"I see your point. Keep going."

"There is something bigger at work here, something sinister. This isn't just some average battle between the white man and the Indians. Whatever is going on, this mission is not likely to be completed in our usual ways. This is not going to be a fist fight/knife fight/sword battle kind of thing. We are going to have to figure out what is going on before we decide what we are going to do."

"Well," I said, "we are starting on day three, which means we are running out of time. Normally we follow my lead, but God has been humbling me a bit over the last several hours, and I'm willing to acknowledge that this time we may need to follow your lead. What do you suggest?"

Carrie looked at me, and the look on her face was utter gratefulness.

"Thank you, Kyle, that means a lot to me. The first thing we need to do is find out what connection this Maya blue dye has to all of this mess. I have a sneaking hunch that it is going to upend a bunch of our history books."

"What do you mean?"

"The standard view of history is that this area was originally settled by Indian tribes like the Creek and the Cherokee and that no other tribes came this far. I have a hunch that might not be the case. If Drew is right about this dye, then it may be that some of the Mayans themselves actually managed to make their way into Georgia."

"But why, Sis? Why come such a long way? And if they were here, or I guess I should say 'are' here, where are they?"

"That, my muscled-up brother, is exactly what we need to find out."

We called Aly in and started day three with prayer. We prayed for safety, of course, but we also prayed for God to give us wisdom and perception to be able to see what we needed to see and know what we needed to know.

When we were done praying, I looked over Carrie and said, "Where to?"

Aly just looked at me like I had lost my mind, but she said nothing.

"We need to find Rain Water; we need to talk to him. Do you think you can track him?"

I grinned. "Does a hot pepperoni pizza have a short lifespan?"

Carrie smiled back, and I stepped out of the darkness into the light, in more ways than one, really. I was determined that this day I would do things God's way, not mine, no matter where it led.

By the time we arrived at the camp where we had seen Rain Water and a few of his people just two days ago, they were gone without a trace, as I suspected they would be.

"Looks like we will have our work cut out for us. I figured that Rain Water would see some sign of our being here and abandon this camp. That means he will also be being doubly careful not to leave any sign of his own passing at this point. Everyone keep your eyes open and be very quiet. Remember that, while we are looking for them, they are now also watching for us."

On the far western side of the campsite, there was a tiny, winding path down the other side of the ridge. It had likely been made by goats and deer and then followed by Indians through the years. The sun was now high in the sky, and each time we walked out from under the boughs of overhead branches, we felt its heat trying to beat us down. It was a constant cycle of sun and shade, sun and shade, but as we descended to lower and lower elevations, the sun and heat grew more sporadic, and the shade and cool more constant.

It was slow going. Not because we could not walk or run fast, we certainly could, but because Rain Water was leaving so little sign for us to follow. Actually, I was pretty sure he was leaving no trace at all, and that any little signs I was seeing were likely caused by the women and children in tow with him.

"If we find them, it will not be for any lack of skill on Rain Water's part," I said, "he is really, really good."

"You got this, big brother," Aly chirped cheerfully.

"Thanks, Squirt. But for now, let's stop and take a few minutes of a lunch break."

Immediately, we all nearly jumped out of our skins as a new voice chimed in, "That is an excellent idea, children, one must be careful not to get famished out here in the wild."

We all whirled to meet the owner of the voice, but even before my "whirl" was completed I had already processed and identified the source of the soothing voice. I knew I had heard it before:

I know you are all angry, and rightly so. Rain Water has cause trouble here yet again.

But it is not just him, he is merely the tip of the spear, so to speak. Your crops are stolen, and your families starve, because of his tribe, not just him...

As I completed my 180-degree spin, my eyes fell once again on a tall, thin man with a slightly misshaped head.

"How did you follow us?" and "Why are you here?" were gushing forth from Carrie and Aly at the exact same time, and both of them sounded slightly panicked. The thin man smiled, and as he did I could feel the fear and apprehension leaving my body. This man had the kindest smile I had ever seen except for maybe that of my own mom. I really liked this guy.

"I am truly sorry," he said, "I did not mean to frighten you. I was not actually following you, I was following Rain Water, or at least attempting to do so. Since you are following him as well, it was inevitable our paths would cross somewhere along the way."

"And what exactly do you want with him?" Carrie asked sternly. I was a bit miffed at her tone, Mom and Dad have taught us to be a lot more polite than that.

"Not what you think, my dear, not what you think," he said sincerely. "It occurred to me after you children left town the other day that the way I worded things has left you with the wrong idea. Everything I said about Rain Water is entirely true. He is a bloodthirsty savage, and yes, most everyone around here would like to see him and his entire tribe destroyed. I, though, think there is a better way. It is clear that we and Rain Water's tribe cannot coexist peacefully. Not as long as we are in the same place. But for all of his murder and violence, I believe that in one way Rain Water is still a man of honor.

"Creek are known to keep their word, at least the warriors among them. I believe that the best way to handle the situation is for me to challenge Rain Water personally. I may seem thin and mild-mannered, but I do have some strength and skill about me. For the good of my people, for the good of this entire valley, I would be willing to risk my life in a fight with Rain Water, as long as he promises to move his entire tribe to another area if I win."

"Would it be a fight to the death?" she snapped.

"Heavens no, dear, not unless he makes it so. I myself have no desire to die, nor do I have any desire to kill. If Rain Water manages to overpower me, I will simply surrender, and we will move. If I manage to overpower him, I will most certainly give him that same option, rather than kill him."

Given my experience in Rogersville with Black Crow, everything the thin man said made perfect sense. I looked over at Carrie and could tell that even my skeptical and suspicious sister was about halfway swayed over to the thin man's position.

"What do you need from us?" I asked.

"Just find him and give him my message. Tell him that I guarantee him safe passage into town for the contest and that if I lose, I will move all of my people to another area, but if he loses he must move all of his people to another area."

"Wouldn't it be easier if we all look for him together?" Aly asked.

The thin man smiled that infinitely kind smile once again, and said, "No, young one, I think not. The more people who go traipsing about after him, the more likely he is to see or hear them coming. And besides, I need to get back into town to attend to the latest chapter in all of this strife, preparing for the funeral tomorrow morning."

That caught me off guard. "What funeral?"

The man began to tremble just a bit, and it seemed as if he was aging before my very eyes. Then he began to sob as he said, "The funeral of my eleven-year-old daughter..."

Chapter Eleven

We watched the thin man leave, and I could see his shoulders rising and falling as he did. I could tell that he was crying and wiping tears as he faded into the trees.

"Wow, that changes everything," I said. "For a little while there I was beginning to think that maybe I had misjudged Rain Water. I know for certain that I misjudged our thin man there. But the good news is, his plan is both a good one and a fair one. And, I might add, for us, it is about the simplest solution we have ever had to one of these adventures. Normally, we are the ones doing the fighting, in this case all we have to do is deliver an invitation."

Carrie, for her part, still looked like she was struggling to process everything. I knew I needed to say something quickly and something smart.

"Look, sis, this makes perfect sense, and it is a foolproof and fair solution. Even if we aren't sure who is right, in this scenario everyone has an opportunity to walk away alive."

"Well," she said grudgingly, "I have to give your logic a high score on that one. And, since we have no better lead to pursue, I suppose this plan is as good as any other."

I was happy. No, scratch that; I was ecstatic. Having Carrie completely on board with any plan always made things go so much simpler. And, though I would never tell her this, the more I thought about a father going back to town to conduct the funeral of his own daughter, the more a bitter hatred welled up inside me. That could've been one of my own sisters; it could have been one of my father's daughters. I hate, hate, hate anyone hurting a girl.

We ate our lunch quickly and then wasted no time swinging into action. I managed to pick up the trail again, and we were back in pursuit of Rain Water and his tribe.

The trail led through a clearing and up into a lovely stand of evergreens. The smell was the most amazing thing you could ever imagine, but I was trying to focus on what my eyes told me rather than what my nose was telling me. A small mushroom with the top knocked off. A twig that had been snapped. A long, black human hair or two hanging on a branch, silently landing there as an Indian passed by.

The trail began to get very strenuous after a while. It led up very steep hills and back down the other side. One moment we had to claw our way up on hands and knees, and the next moment we had to form a human rope to make our way safely back down.

Then it clicked with me: Rain Water knew he was being pursued, and he was intentionally taking the most difficult paths to slow that pursuit!

"That sly devil," I said with an admiring grin, "he may be a savage, but he is definitely not a dummy."

Our pathway led across a plateau just below the ridge of one of the mountains. It was level walking for about a half mile, with towering trees every few feet to weave through. It reminded me a lot of Cattail Peak on Mount Mitchell in North Carolina, on the Deep Gap Trail. My dad loves to take us hiking there whenever we are home.

The level walk did not last long though, for very soon we were heading down yet another steep embankment.

"This is hard walking, big brother," Aly said as she huffed and puffed just a bit.

"I know, sis, I know. But we have been through worse. Let's just keep at it, we are still most definitely on the right trail."

Rain Water was clearly picking up the pace. I knew that he knew that he was being followed. The good part about that was, a person who hurries in the wilderness makes mistakes, and that makes it easier to follow him.

I was right in the middle of thinking that thought and admiring my own tracking skills when it all came home to me very clearly: I was the one who had gotten in a hurry and made the mistake.

Something about being yanked off of your feet and finding yourself dangling in midair with a rope around your ankle will make that kind of thing fairly clear to you.

Carrie and Aly instinctively rushed to me and assumed a defensive posture around me, not sure of what was happening, or why I was suddenly upside down.

"Kyle!" Carrie screamed.

Before I could answer, Rain Water stepped out from behind a tree, bow in hand, arrow at the ready.

"Please," I pleaded, "don't hurt my sisters; it's me you want."

Rain Water's eyes narrowed to slits. Then he pulled back on the bow with all his might and let the arrow fly.

Chapter Twelve

You know how they say that when you're about to die your entire life flashes before your eyes? Not true. Not true at all. The only thought that ran through my mind was, "I'm going to wet my pants upside down, and then die like that. Not cool." Mind you, it only took about 1/1000 of a second for that thought to run through my mind. And it only took about another 1/1000 of a second for me to feel the thud of my head against the ground.

Carrie had screamed and then instantly cut it short.

Aly had not screamed, she had gasped, but then I immediately heard her say, "Whoa! Best! Shot! Ever!"

Best shot ever? Did she really just say that? I began to feel all over my chest to see if an arrow was sticking out of it, but there was nothing. As my eyes refocused, I looked up and could see half a rope still swinging from the tree above me. I looked down, and the other half was still tied securely about my ankle.

Yep. Best shot ever indeed.

I slowly sat up and turned to face the big Indian, who by this point had another arrow already at the ready. Everything grew ominously quiet as he and I locked eyes. Finally, I broke the silence.

"Thank you. You had me dead to rights. You could have killed me, but you didn't. But why didn't you?"

"I do not shed innocent blood, young white brave. I want nothing more than to do as I have always done; to live in peace in these hills with my people."

"Well if you aren't the one shedding blood, then who is?"

"I do not know," he said matter-of-factly. "I do know that the white man will always blame the Indian first and that he will kill him without ever inquiring of the truth. We are savages to you, less than human. My entire tribe could be wiped out, and no one among the white man would care. But I care. And though I do not wish to shed blood, I will do whatever is needed to keep my people safe."

As I brushed myself off and stood to my feet, I smiled at Rain Water and said, "In that case, I bring good news. The gentleman in town who seems to be running things has proposed a contest to settle the issue. He assures you safe passage if you will come into town and face him. He is willing to fight you, man-to-man, face-to-face, and whoever loses must move his people from the area. He sent me here with that message."

Rain Water's countenance changed instantly, and he spat on the ground in anger. "He assures it, does he? I do not wish to offend you, young white warrior, but the assurances of the white man are a shaky foundation indeed. Our lands have been stolen despite assurances from the white man. Our women and children have been taken despite assurances from the white man. Our people have been imprisoned despite assurances from the white man. The assurances of the white man, young white warrior, mean nothing to me."

Honestly, I was pretty offended right at that moment. He was talking about my people. I opened my mouth to defend them, to defend me, but the words died in my throat as the shot rang out through the trees.

The bow and arrow went flying from Rain Water's hands as the bullet slammed into his chest just below his right shoulder.

God is so good to have allowed us so many adventures before this one; that previous training made it possible for me to act instantly out of pure instinct. I lunged forward, grabbed Rain Water as he dropped to his knees and pulled him over the other side of the hill with me. He and I went tumbling down about thirty feet, and in the midst of all the tumbling, I was able to see Carrie and Aly sliding down behind us, and Aly had Rain Water's bow in her hands. God bless them, those sisters of mine could spring into action instantly and somehow always manage to get everything right.

I didn't know what was happening yet. But I did know that a man who could have killed me but didn't had just been shot from a distance by someone hiding in the trees. That was not cool with me, not cool at all. Before we ever got to the bottom of our tumble down the hill, I had already made up my mind to get him to safety until I could work all of this out.

We hit the bottom, and I grabbed Rain Water and got him up onto his feet, putting his left arm around my shoulders. Carrie grabbed him from the other side, and we were off and running with Aly right behind us.

Despite his blood loss, Rain Water moved with the urgency of a man who knew that his life is on the line. As we ran, through gasping breath I hissed, "Where can we go to hide? You know these mountains far better than we."

Rain Water was spitting blood as he tried to speak. I knew that was a bad sign, a very bad sign.

"Half a day's journey," he gasped, "near the top of the mountain calling to the sun."

I looked ahead and saw the mountain that the sun was dropping toward and would reach in a few hours. If we hurried, we might just make it before nightfall.

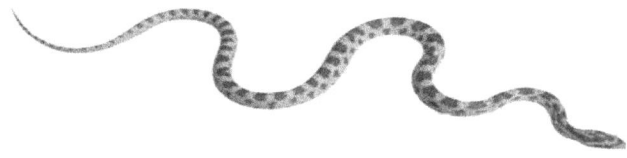

We had been going hard and fast for about two hours, and the light was almost gone. Rain Water was now barely able to support any of his own weight, and Carrie and I were really struggling with him. I had looped my right arm around his waist and was trying to take as much of the weight as I could, knowing my strength was substantially greater than my sister's. But nonetheless, all three of us were almost done in.

Aly, for her part, was bringing up the rear, the bow in one hand, and arrow in the other, ready to protect us from whatever or whoever was chasing us. Though I was exhausted, I still managed a smile as I thought of the misfortune that would come to anyone who underestimated this pint-sized sister of mine holding that oversized bow and arrow. If they got within fifty yards of her, I knew she could put an arrow dead center of their chest.

"There," Rain Water said weakly as he pointed ahead and to the left. And sure enough, about seventy-five yards up the steep hill we had been climbing was a tiny cabin nestled against the base of the cliff. We picked up the pace and rushed toward it, though "rushed" would be a very relative term since we were all spent. As we came, I was doing my best to evaluate the defensibility of the setting.

Not good.

"We really need to hope we have managed to throw off any pursuit," I said to whoever was listening. "This cabin does not look to provide a way out in the back, and therefore, it is as much a trap as it is a fortress.

A well-armed contingent could hold people off for a very long time, but I don't think we qualify at the moment."

Rain Water groaned in pain as we clip-clopped up the two stairs, onto the porch, and to the front door. I reached for the handle and found it locked firm. Rain Water groaned again, and through parched lips said, "Leave me here, young warrior, I am not strong enough to open the door."

"You may not be, but I am."

Carrie and I carefully laid Rain Water on the porch. I could have simply broken a window, but I wanted to leave those intact as long as I could to provide a place of warmth for Rain Water during what could be a cold Georgia night. Wood, I could patch. Glass, I could not.

Three kicks. Dad could have done it in one, but I still wasn't too displeased with the effort.

We got everyone inside, and I shoved an old rustic chair up against the door to keep it shut. Everything in the cabin was covered in about an eighth of an inch of dust; it had not been used for many years. There were two rooms, the main room we just broke into and a small room in the back. There was also a fireplace and some firewood carefully stacked beside it put there by who knows who and who knows when.

"What now, Kyle?"

The groan from the corner answered her question. Rain Water was in trouble.

"We have to get that wound taken care of," I said, "and quickly."

Carrie and Aly worked to get Rain Water up onto a small cot in the back room. I begin to arrange some small kindling in the fireplace.

As the girls came back in and saw what I was doing, Aly's eyes grew wide, and she said, "Is that a good idea? The smoke rising from the chimney will give away our location as effectively as if we put up a neon sign."

"I know, I know. But we absolutely don't have any choice on this one. I have to get that bullet out, and I will have to sterilize a knife to do it."

Once I had the kindling in place, I reached into my night pack and got some matches. The kindling quickly blazed to life, and as we blew on it, I added larger and larger pieces. Soon there was a respectable fire going; I was able to turn my attention to the next part of the procedure.

I took my knife from the side pocket of my jeans and placed the blade in the hot coals. After a few moments it was glowing red, and I knew it was ready.

I used a rag, which we wet from a spring just behind the house, to grab the handle and pull out the knife. Then I walked over to the big Indian.

"Rain Water," I need to get that bullet out, and then I need to cauterize the wound, or you will die. Do you trust me and can you take the pain?"

The big Indian looked up at me, and even in his weakened state mustered a smile. "You have risked your life to bring me here. I trust you. But if you ever ask me if I can take pain again, I shall kill you."

He smiled a bit bigger as he said that, and I knew that he was sort of kidding, but only partly. Indians pride themselves on being able to take any pain that can be dished out to them.

I grimaced as I ripped open the top of his chest covering and saw the nasty wound that I was dealing with. There were already black streaks starting to spread out from it, and I knew that he was likely to die from infection if I didn't find a way to stop it.

My hands trembled as I moved the knife toward the wound. Seeing this kind of thing on old westerns on TV is a lot different from doing it in real life. As I slid the knife down into the wound Rain Water grimaced and clenched the sides of the cot but made not a sound.

Sweat was pouring from my forehead and from his within a matter of seconds as I dug around trying to get to the bullet. Finally, I felt it. I kept the knife firmly in place, and, fighting back the desire to throw up, I slid my left index finger down into the hole and pinched the bullet between it and the blade. I slowly pulled it out, and as I did Rain Water finally exhaled. He had been holding his breath.

Me? I passed out cold on the floor.

When I came to, there was a wet rag on my forehead, and as I looked down at my left hand, I realized that it had been cleaned.

"I gotcha, bro," Carrie said with a smile. "You did good. Mom and dad have always suspected that I would be the doctor in the family, but it looks like you may have a bright future in the surgical field yourself!"

I grinned weakly and said, "Sure, because every good doctor passes out right after he finishes surgery."

I sat up and looked over at Rain Water, and he was resting, albeit fitfully.

"Kyle, we do have a bit of a problem."

Carrie motioned to the window, and I could see that there was no light coming through it.

"Right. It's time for our nightly trip home, and yet Rain Water is being pursued by someone who clearly has every intention of killing him without the least amount of due process."

As the three of us huddled together and tried to figure out what to do, the big Indian spoke weakly. "Come, children, come to me for a moment."

We walked over to him, and he looked up at us with grateful eyes. "Go," he said. "You are not safe here. Whoever is hunting me will not hesitate to kill you as well, and I am too weak to defend you. Go, and be safe, and know that you have the gratitude of a warrior of the Creek Indians."

"Rain Water," I said, "we are going to go, but we are also going to return. I cannot explain it to you, but we must make our way out into the woods for the night. We are going to do some things to hopefully keep you safe while we are gone, and tomorrow I promise you we will return."

And with that, we turned and walked out into the night.

Chapter Thirteen

As I lay in my bunk at camp Hosanna, my mind was positively racing. We had set up some surprises for anyone who got too close to Rain Water's cabin. I just hoped they would be enough to scare off any attackers until we could get back with some help or some answers or both.

I had to put all of that out of my mind, though, because the day was starting fast and furious once again at camp.

We all got up and rushed down to breakfast and found an amazing selection of waffles and toppings. Man, let me tell you, there is nothing like sugar and white flour carbohydrates to make already hyper teenagers even more so. We laughed and cut up and had an excellent time, and we even took a few minutes to play some carpet ball.

If you have never played carpet ball before, it is a wooden trough about eighteen inches wide and twelve feet or so long. You use pool balls, one person sets his or hers up on his side the other one does so on theirs, and then you use the cue ball, rolling it back and forth to see who can be the first one to knock all of his opponents balls into the tray at the end.

This morning I was challenged by Brother Abbott's spunky daughter, Prissy. I smiled and gave her the first roll.

Do you know how embarrassing it is to be beaten at anything by a ten-year-old girl? Especially one who doesn't mind at all rubbing it in? That kid was good!

"Nice job, girl," I said being as complimentary as I could through my wounded pride.

"Of course it's a nice job," she said. "If you like, later on, I can give you some lessons on how it's done!"

Twenty kids around us burst out laughing, and most of them were pointing fingers at me. Including Carrie and Aly. Traitors.

I smiled and nodded my head to her as if to say, "Not bad, not bad at all."

After that everyone rushed back to the cabins for cleaning time, while the staff reset everything in the meeting hall for the morning service. We all came back down, and the service got started, Olivia Abbott led a group of about ten counselors in a song, she played the guitar and sang lead while they sang harmony along with her. It was really very good. Then it was time for dad to preach, and this time in his series on the life of Sampson he preached a message called, "The High Cost of Low Living."

Sampson, bless his ignorant soul, continued to dabble in sin over and over again despite all of the warning signs he was being given. It ended up costing him his eyes, his freedom, everything that really mattered. As I thought about it, I could not help but wonder why people are so incredibly stubborn, and why they cannot seem to grasp the law of sowing and reaping.

Galatians 6:7-8 says, "Be not deceived; God is not mocked: for whatsoever a man soweth, that shall he also reap. For he that soweth to his flesh shall of the flesh reap corruption; but he that soweth to the Spirit shall of the Spirit reap life everlasting."

For every action, there is a consequence, good or bad. If you pray, you get closer to God. If you drink alcohol, you destroy brain cells, get bad breath, destroy your health, and have a hard time staying employed.

If you read the Bible, you grow wise. If you do drugs, you end up stealing to support your habit; you become a liar, a thief, and ruin your family.

If you stay a virgin until you get married, you have a priceless gift to present to your spouse, and he or she will likely never worry about your loyalty to them. If you give up your virginity before marriage, your spouse knows that you didn't care enough about them to wait, and they may even wonder whether or not you will continue to be faithful to them.

The invitation was a good one, with most every kid in camp crowding around the altar praying, asking God to help them to make the right decisions in every aspect of their lives. I love, I just love invitations like that.

Once the service was done and the invitation was concluded, we went back out to the playing field for a Camp Hosanna original: eggs in a basket. It could best be described as something as violent as a hockey fight while being as funny as a really bad opera.

Basically, there's a huge circle, some trash cans on the inside of it, a bunch of balls, a couple of people on offense trying to get the balls into the trash cans, and a greater number of people on defense trying to keep them from doing so. There is a lot of tackling, fighting, pushing and shoving. Basically just good clean fun that results in bandages and maybe a few stitches here or there.

While I was playing, though, I couldn't help but notice that, once again, Carrie was taking time to speak to Drew. And once again, though I knew she was probably doing so for the best of reasons, I could feel that same anger welling up inside of me.

Hey, this is Carrie, I'll pick up the story from here. At a break in the girl's game, I sauntered over to Drew and sat down beside him.

"Hey, Drew, would you mind if I pick your brain a little bit?"

He seemed pretty surprised at that. I'm guessing from the way he shies away from people and acts like a whipped puppy all the time, probably not many people have ever been nice to him or told him that he was of much worth. But, as brilliant as I am, I am also smart enough to know that sometimes, God has prepared others with even better knowledge of a subject than I have, and it is wise to be humble enough to seek that knowledge out when needed. This was one of those times.

"Uh, yeah, sure. What can I help you with?"

"Well, you were talking about that Maya blue. There are some things I, um, remember from somewhere, and since you seem to know something about the Mayans I was curious as to whether or not you could help me understand what they mean."

He raised his eyebrows in a bit of surprise, and said, "Okay, I'll sure do my best. What is it you remember?"

"Maybe it would be best if I drew it for you, no pun intended."

He smiled a bit at and then slid a napkin over to me. I picked up a box of crayons one of the staff member's kids had left on the other end of the table and begin to draw as best as I could remember the sequence of pictures on the wall in the cave. When I was done, I slid the napkin over to Drew, and said, "This."

Drew's eyes got wide; he was clearly impressed, either for the good or for the bad. For the longest time, he sat there and silently studied it symbol by symbol, and then finally he spoke.

"I may not be giving the exact details, but I can tell you that this rings a bell. I can also tell you that it has to do with this area, and seems to be tied in with something I remember from an obscure history documentary. Here goes:

"This flat line with flowers and grass is the symbol for a meadow. The name Hiawassee is often described as the derivative of a similar Cherokee word meaning "meadow." But, the Cherokee and Creek's own history describes the region as being originally occupied by snake idol worshipers, people named the Itza. The Itza Maya in Mexico were known as 'the Children of the Serpent.' In the Itsati language, Hiawassee literally means 'Children of the Pit Viper.'

"The circle of crossing spears alternating red and yellow indicates a conflict, a never ending struggle. But then comes the serpent rising out of the blue ashes, and on the other side of that serpent all of the red spheres are still in the circle, but the yellow spears are broken into pieces and laying below them.

"The rising of the serpent turned the tide of battle, and one people were wiped out completely, the other people thrived and went on to continue their warring ways.

"The pit viper was a powerful god among the Mayans. This is a prophecy that he would rise to power, and the fact that he did so out of the blue ashes meant that he would do so because of the sacrifices given to him, thus the Maya blue color that sacrifices were painted with before they were killed.

"This snake would kill as most snakes do; with a quick and unexpected strike, subtlety, a bite to the leg when his opponent never saw it coming.

"In a nutshell, whoever this pit viper was, if he ever did rise, he would do a lot of damage before he was ever found out.

"What is it that your dad was saying during the invitation last night about the subtlety of the serpent in the garden of Eden, and the damage he did to mankind through it, and the damage he still desires to do by tricking us? It sounds sort of similar to all this, doesn't it?"

"Yes, it certainly does," I said. In the back of my mind, I was processing everything he said while at the same time being pleasantly and thoroughly surprised at the fact that not only was he listening to my dad preaching, but he could actually repeat back to me what he had said. In addition to the nighttime adventure we were facing, I was hoping God would bring about the greatest adventure of all: seeing this precious young man get whatever he needed from God.

"Tell me one more thing," I asked. "Is there anything in all of these drawings that tell us how to defeat, I mean, that would tell how the pit viper could be beaten?"

Drew sort of cocked his head at my little slip of the lip there, but shook it off and answered, "No. This seems to have been drawn very much from his perspective. In this series of pictures, the serpent is pretty much all-powerful and always wins."

I told Drew thank you for the help and went back out onto the field to join the rest of my cabin mates, but in my mind, I was mumbling to myself, "Then we'll just have to find a way to change that drawing."

And then I went and found dad; I needed to talk to him, and fast.

This is Kyle again. I'll pick the story back up from here. The rest of the afternoon passed uneventfully, with a lot of games and laughter. Supper, as always, was fantastic. This time camp president Stan Wood had prepared an incredible barbecue meal. It reminded me of something my dad always says; "If God didn't intend us to eat animals, He wouldn't have made pigs taste like bacon."

For service that night, dad preached "The Difference Between Convictions and Conformity." It is from 2 Chronicles 24 and is the story of young King Joash. He became king when he was just seven years old. As long as the high priest lived, he always did right. But once the high priest died, he became wicked. Him doing right was dependent on someone else. All he had was a conformity to an outward standard; he did not have any inner convictions that drove him to always do right.

115

Influence to do right from the outside is good, but having an inner determination to do right, being directed by the Holy Spirit to do right and listening to Him, that is 1,000 times better. I hit the altar that night, praying that God will always help me to have the convictions to do right, even if I was standing alone.

The altar was crowded as usual, and several more got saved that night. We went out into the open field to have our devotions as a cabin and then went back to the cabins for some sleep. Or in my case, our case, we Night Heroes, a trip back into the past where would hopefully find a big Indian waiting for us in a little cabin way up in the hills and some answers to the questions still swirling around in my mind.

Chapter Fourteen

"Good morning, Night Heroes, welcome to day four of your adventure."

We all sat up and brushed the sleep out of our eyes as we responded to the kind voice of our Conductor.

"Good morning, sir," Aly chirped cheerfully. "We missed you yesterday. Was Dunkin' Donuts running a special you just could not resist?"

The Conductor kept a stone face, and said, "Young lady, I think you know where I am from."

He left that statement just hanging there for a couple of awkward seconds, and then smiled from ear to ear and said, "We have Krispy Kreme."

All three of us erupted in laughter at that. Good way to start the day!

"In all seriousness, there will be a day or two here or there in your adventures when I am perhaps needed elsewhere. You are experienced enough now to know what to do, so just do it. Now, what are your plans for this day?"

"We pray first, and then I think we have to head back to that cabin in the hills to check on Rain Water."

"Maybe," he said. "But please keep something in mind. Not all enemies are straightforward in their approach. Some, in fact, are incredibly subtle. Knowledge of that fact will be a good compass to steer by.

"Godspeed on this day, children."

And with that, our Conductor once again walked out of the cave into the bright light of the rising sun and faded from sight.

We Warner kids, the Night Heroes, once again knelt together before the Lord and lifted our voices up to him in earnest prayer. How could we ever walk a step without Him, and how much less could we be the heroes He has called us to be without His help every step of the way?

Once we finished praying, we sat up and discussed our plans for the day.

Hey, this is Carrie again. I will take over for just a few minutes here, to let you know what was going on in my head, and why.

Once we finished praying and began to discuss our plans for the day, I did something I do not normally do. I misled my brother just a bit. Actually, no, I am pretty sure I actually led him just right, it's just that I couldn't do so directly, I had to do so in a round-about way. There really wasn't much of another option, as far as I could tell.

"Kyle, I know we need to get up to check on Rain Water, but let's do one other thing first. Someone is out there trying to kill him, and whoever it is isn't letting himself be known or seen. I think we need some help on this one, and there is one person who seems better connected than most anyone else.

"I know he will be attending to the funeral, so let's go pay our respects, then afterward let's see if we can speak to him. He said the funeral was this morning. We move fast enough that we can get there for it, speak to him, and still get back to Rain Water by mid-afternoon."

Kyle looked at me, clearly impressed.

"Good thought, sis, I like it. Let's move."

Yes, Kyle, I thought, *let's move indeed...*

Carrie's idea was a good one, and I was happy to oblige her. If we could enlist the help of the thin man, our odds of figuring all of this out were much greater. We made our way down the mountain once again and back down the Unicoi Trail. In no time flat, we were traipsing into town once more, where, it would be logical to assume, the funeral would be taking place.

As we stepped into town and I looked around, my habit of keeping my eyes and ears opened for anything abnormal kicked into high gear, because something was definitely odd in the most normal of ways. Yeah, I know that sounds weird, but it is about the best way to describe it.

What I mean is, for a town about to be having the funeral of a man's daughter, nothing seemed very funeral like. In fact, nothing seemed different at all. People were walking from place to place, talking on porches, going about as if everything was business as usual.

For some reason, before anyone saw us, I grabbed Carrie and Aly and pulled them aside, out of sight, behind a building.

"Okay, something doesn't seem right. For a town that should be mourning the loss of the little girl of a prominent citizen, things seem remarkably normal. What say ye?"

Carrie and Aly both agreed. We finally decided to go around behind the buildings and make our way hopefully unseen and unheard to the backside of the inn. That entailed a whole lot of tiptoeing and ducking down below windows, tiptoeing again and ducking down behind another window, until finally we arrived at the still broken window in the back of the inn.

We could hear voices from inside talking, all men as far as I could tell. The voices seem to be overlapping, talking one over top of the other, which was both bad manners and very frustrating for me, since I really couldn't make out with any coherency what was being said or what the main topic of conversation was. There were certain words that seem to be recurring over and over; Indian, problem, posse, things like that. Finally, though, a rather familiar voice spoke up (though "up" does not really do it justice, as it was both as low and seemingly calm as ever), and everyone else fell quiet.

"We all know what must be done. For the sake of our wives and children, Rain Water and his entire tribe must be wiped out before some child ends up being killed."

"And how do you propose that we do that?" came a nasally voice of a seemingly very old man. "We can't even track him; he's too good out in the wilderness."

"We don't have to," the thin man said, and as he said it, you could almost hear the smile that he said it through, "others have already done that for us. We have only to gather a suitable force, and we can take them all. We will begin with his ragtag band of a tribe, whose whereabouts I have already determined since they are far less skilled in the woods than he. They are separated from him and will not be much of a problem. Half a day's hike from here will bring us up on them, and if we strike fast enough, they will not so much as have time to put an arrow to a bow. That will be the task for today.

"The task for tomorrow will be to climb the hill and, at our leisure destroy Rain Water himself."

"What then?" came the question from a man with a bit of a Hispanic sound. "Will the prophecy finally be fulfilled?"

"My brethren," the thin man said with what sounded like greatly mounting pleasure, "the time of the fulfilling of the prophecy is indeed upon us. We will smite down our enemies, the serpent will arise, and all will worship. All of you, all of you shall be my children...the children of the Pit Viper!"

I could not help it. I had to get at least a peek of what was happening at that moment, so I stuck my head up just a touch in the corner of the broken window. I could see that Carrie and Aly were down low and were looking through cracks in the wood.

The thin man had removed the hat from his head, and I could see that it was horribly misshapen. It looked as if it came almost to a point in the back. The man's dark skin almost seemed to be glowing, and he had an evil look in his eyes that almost seemed reptilian. He was holding his hands out to the side as his face was turned toward the heaven, and he was basking in the worship of all the men in that room, who were now bowing in a circle around him.

We were in trouble. Rain Water was in trouble. All of his people were in trouble. And it was all my fault.

Chapter Fifteen

I made a hand motion to my sisters, and we very quietly moved about thirty feet back up into the trees. Whispering, oh so quietly, I said, "Guys, I have blown it. I was so fixed on Rain Water being the bad guy just because he is an Indian and so convinced that the thin man was a good guy that I have wasted valuable time and have now put a lot of people in jeopardy."

"Carrie, do you have any idea what in the world this prophecy/children of the pit viper thing is all about?"

"As a matter of fact I do," she whispered back.

She gave me a quick tutorial to bring me up to speed on what she had learned from Drew. I groaned inside as I heard it, realizing that I had most likely misjudged Drew just as bad as I had Rain Water. And why? For no good reason other than that he was from the north and wore a long sleeved leather jacket in the middle of the summer.

"What are we going to do?" Aly asked. "Rain Water is expecting us if he isn't already dead, and yet his people are about to be attacked and wiped out. To make matters worse, we don't even know where they are."

I grimaced, not liking what I was about to suggest. "As much as I hate to say it, this may be another Germany scenario."

"Divide and conquer?" Carrie asked.

"Looks like it," I said. "You two need to get to Rain Water as fast as you can and do what you can to keep him alive and healthy. Make sure he stays hydrated. Get some vitamins into him. Let him know what we have discovered and make the place as defensible as you can."

"What about you, and what about his people?" Carrie said with obvious concern.

"My plan on that," I whispered back, "is to return the favor on our slithering serpent in there. He followed us; I intend to follow him."

"And do what," Aly said with a twisted up face, "fight all of them?"

"No, certainly not. My hope is to be able to cause enough of a ruckus at just the right time to get Rain Water's people running before they can be slaughtered."

"And how do you intend to do that?"

I grinned. "Oh, just a few extra things I bought from Brother Abbott yesterday..."

Hey, this is Aly. I'll pick up my and Carrie's part of the story from here for the time being.

We had all sat quietly back in the trees for about an hour until the posse had gathered, organized, and set off in pursuit of Rain Water's people.

It was a huge group, probably fifty or better. That worried me, a lot, for Kyle's sake. If any of those fifty realized that he was following them, he would be dead for sure. But knowing my brother, and how skilled he can be when he really focuses, I knew that he stood an above average chance of following them without being detected.

Once Kyle had started after them, Carrie and I went the other direction as fast as we could go working our way back to the cabin on the side of the mountain. The day was hot and very muggy. Honestly, it almost felt like the devil was breathing his foul breath out on us. That would figure, since either directly or indirectly he had to be behind all of this madness. Anytime someone other than God is worshiped, the devil certainly has a hand in it.

Our legs were burning, and we were puffing for air by the time we arrived. It had taken us about three hours at a solid pace. The noisemakers we had left the night before hooked up with fishing line were still intact. If anyone had come anywhere near the cabin, they would surely have tripped one of them, and likely been scared away. So we knew that while the serpent may have observed the cabin from a distance, neither he nor anyone else actually came all the way to it.

We came out into the open and made for the cabin, fearing for what would find inside. I was hoping and praying our big friendly Indian was still alive. But as we walked in the door, I was not so sure. There was a big lump still on the cot, but no movement whatsoever.

Carrie and I rushed over to him, and as we shook him a little we heard a pitiful groan. I tell you, that is one of the prettiest sounds I have ever heard.

"Rain Water," Carrie said gently, "we need you to sit up. We have some things to help you."

The Indian just groaned, and through raspy breath said, "Do my people live?"

Carrie and I just looked at each other, and then as she looked back at him, she said, "My brother is going after them right now to try and keep them safe. Please, sit up, we need to get some water and vitamins into you."

With a lot of effort, she and I managed to get him into a seated position. I tell you that big Indian was very heavy and very solid.

We got him to drink, very slowly, so that he would not choke. I had brought a bottle of water with me in my pack from our time. We also got some vitamin C into him, which my grandmother swears by. She says it helps the immune system. Carrie then got him to eat a bit of trail mix. We needed this man to live, and then needed him to get some strength back, and fast.

This is Kyle. Let me tell you how things were going with my part of the mission. When the posse had set out on their mission of destruction, they did not realize they had a tagalong coming behind them. I made sure to keep a distance of about seventy-five yards between them and me; I did not want them to know I was there.

My heart sank as we went farther and farther, for one very important reason: they were going directly opposite from the direction that my sisters were going. Depending on how far they went until we reached our destination, I knew that I might not be able to get back to my sisters by nightfall. We had not even discussed that possibility.

The posse was moving without speaking; everyone was following the pointy-headed slithering devil out in front of them.

I was angry, so bitterly, coldly angry that I allowed myself to be so deceived. But, like my dad always says, "the best way to fix the problem is to fix the problem." Yes, I know, that sounds like circular reasoning. But it actually makes perfect sense. In this case, I could either sit back and mope and whine about my mistake, or I could do what was necessary to fix the mistake.

We were moving at a pretty good clip. From time to time, the thin man would hold up his hand, and everyone would come to a stop while he examined some evidence of Indians passing that way. As he did so now, I could hear someone near the back of the line say, "We should be on them before the sun peaks in the sky."

I looked up and realized that if he were correct, we were likely no more than a half hour away. I took a few deep breaths as I contemplated what I was going to be attempting to do. I knew that I would have to be successful in both phases: the doing and the escaping. And with the posse of fifty or so people, that escaping part might prove more difficult than I could imagine.

I smiled, though, as I looked down at my feet. In a "chase-me contest" through the woods, I would give the upper hand to my sneakers over their boots any day.

The posse moved forward again and once more I fell in behind them unseen. Everyone was moving slower now, and much quieter. That told me that we must be getting very close by the thin man's estimation.

Timing would be everything. I needed to give Rain Water's people enough time and enough of a head start to get away, but I did not want to spring my plan too early, lest we be too far away for them to get the message.

Since I didn't know where they were, or how close or how far away, and yet needed to be perfect in my timing, I did the best thing I knew to do: I prayed.

Lord, please forgive me for my stubbornness and hardheadedness. You know what I need to do, and you also know that I don't know exactly when I need to do it. But the timing needs to be just right. Lord, please speak to my heart, please let me know exactly when to do it, not a moment too soon, not a moment too late. This I pray in Jesus name, Amen.

I kid you not, we took about fifteen more steps, and it's as if the Holy Spirit Himself spoke one word very clearly and unmistakably to my heart: "now."

Without a moment's hesitation, I reached into my pack and pulled out a Screaming Dragon, the massive multistage firework I had bought from Brother Abbott. I grabbed a lighter, lit the fuse, and then stepped behind a tree and put a finger in each ear.

As soon as the fuse hit the powder, it sounded like the entire mountain was under assault by the 82nd airborne. Instantly I was out into the open and running with all my might. I did not care if I was seen, in fact, it would be better if I was. I would rather have them following me than following some scared Indians who didn't know what to do.

Boom! Boom! Kablam! Whoosh! Boom Boom Boom Boom! Those fireworks were echoing off the hills and filling the sky, and I knew that Rain Water's people would be scared to death, and running the opposite direction of the noise.

The Boom! Boom! Kablam! Whoosh! Boom Boom Boom Boom! I did not mind. But the Bam Bam Bam of the guns being fired behind me I did mind. As the bark splintered all around me, I knew I definitely had that posse's attention!

I also, at that moment, knew that I was not going to be leading them back to that cabin. I was going to run till nightfall and hopefully stay just far enough ahead of them to keep from being caught or killed, just close enough to them to keep them chasing. I had an advantage; at nightfall, they would be stuck wherever they were, and I would get a free trip home.

Chapter Sixteen

Hey, this is Carrie. As the moments of the day fell away like sands through an hourglass, I grew more and more concerned about my impetuous brother. I knew that he was really upset, and I hoped he wouldn't do anything rash to try and make up for his mistake.

"Do you think he's coming?" Aly asked as she slid up beside me and looked through the window.

"I don't know, sis, I don't know."

"Let's go look for him then."

"No! Absolutely not. We are not going to risk leaving Rain Water alone, or missing Kyle somewhere out in the woods while he's headed this way and we are headed out to who knows where to look for him. If he's not here by nightfall, we take our nightly trip home, and we trust God with him and plan on meeting him back in camp tomorrow morning."

I said it very firmly. But in my heart, I was heading down that same path that Aly was so desperate to be on. My heart, my heart which Jeremiah 17:9 says is desperately wicked and deceitful above all things, was telling me the opposite of what my mind knew was the right answer.

This is Kyle again. As I sat on a rock outcropping with my back against the cool granite, I knew I was probably twelve to fifteen miles away from my sisters. In the last two hours, I had intentionally picked up the pace so severely that all pursuit fell far behind me. I was now watching the sun dip down below the far lovely mountains, kissing our side of the earth goodbye for the night, and allowing the moon to take over in its absence.

"And the lesser light to rule the night," I murmured.

And with that, I closed my eyes, prayed for my sisters to be safe, and went peacefully off to sleep.

It seemed that morning came way too early on this Friday at Camp Hosanna. It was with mixed emotions and also a bit of trepidation that I made my way to the breakfast hall. The mixed emotions were those of the normal kid in me, not wanting camp to end, and the trepidation was from the nervous Night Hero in me, wanting desperately to see my sisters and know that they were okay.

A quick glance into the meeting hall allowed me to meet the dark brown eyes of Carrie and the lighter brown eyes of Aly; eyes all the way around for all three of us that held nothing but relief. We could not talk about it right now, but the unspoken words passed between us anyway as if by thought; *one more night, can we save him?*

After another typically delicious Camp Hosanna breakfast, it was back to the cabins for one more time of cleaning, then back to the meeting hall for one more morning service.

Dad preached his last message on the life of Samson, *Don't Die with the Philistines.* A couple more kids got saved, and a bunch of

Christian kids were crowded around the altar praying for a life that would be both lived right and died right.

The afternoon was a bit more laid back than the rest of the week. We had tons of free time to play carpet ball, volleyball, go tubing, or just kick back and fellowship.

That night, there was no preaching service, there was a fun night/who-won-the-week revelation. The fun time was utterly epic; the Camp Hosanna staff (including the two bacon girls... hard to explain, you would just have to see it) are just crazy, in the best kind of way.

Sadly, my team did not win, but we did come in a close second. It kind of gnawed on me a bit that if I had said a few more verses, we might actually have won. Next year I will fix that.

Soon, though, it was time for a fireside service. Brother Abbott gathered everyone around and spoke to them for a while, and then gave a chance for testimonies. That was amazing; sixteen kids testified that they got saved this week.

But that was not the best part. Not by a long shot. How could it get better than sixteen kids getting saved? Well, let me tell you how...

As one kid after another testified of getting saved, apparently God was hard at work on number seventeen. God is good like that; He never stops drawing souls, even when we least expect it, and of whom we least expect it.

"Um, 'scuse me, but, ah, I was wondering, all these guys are getting saved and all, do yuse guys think maybe I could do that?"

Tears. I immediately felt hot tears streaming down my face. I put my face in my hands, fell to the ground, and immediately asked God to forgive me for being such a lousy witness to Drew, and thanking God for saving him in spite of me. Without even looking, I knew that wherever in the crowd they were, Carrie and Aly were crying too.

I stayed on my face for the longest time, until I heard one of the cabin counselors, a great guy named Garrett, let out a happy yell. I knew then that he had been the one privileged to take his Bible and lead Drew to the Lord.

"Hey everybody," Garrett shouted, "Drew has something to say."

Everyone got utterly quiet, as Drew awkwardly began. I knew he was nervous; his northern accent was way more pronounced than normal.

"Um, ah, I just wanted to say tanks for letting me come, and, uh, for introducing me to Jesus. I wanted to get saved earlier in the week, but I wadn't sure it was okay."

I was a bit stumped at that one, but I kept listening quietly. I had a hunch he was about to explain what he meant by that.

"Um, I ain't been to no church before I moved down heeya. But all da folks at Cohnastone was real nice to me, and dey brought me to camp dis week. Um, before I heard about Jesus, I was, well, a bad kid. Um, yuse guys have seen me wearing dis coat all week. Um, it's, well, here is why I didn't know if it was okay for me ta get saved."

Drew pulled off his coat, and I saw that his arms were covered in tattoos, some of them pretty bad; pentagrams, goat heads, devilish kind of stuff.

"I wanted to tank Carrie, from our church. She took time to talk to me and to be nice to me dis week. And I guess it finally clicked with me, if da preacher's kid ain't embarrassed to be nice to me, I guess God ain't neitha, even if I do got tattoos."

I started bawling again. If it had been up to me, Drew would have likely gone to hell. But my sister was Christ-like enough to him that he was able to conclude that God wouldn't turn him away. I found out later that Drew's parents were actually Satanists when he was younger, thus accounting for the kind of ink he had on his arms. Now they were just agnostic, but still very much lost. He had been coming to church by himself.

    I lay in bed awake for a while that night, even though I knew I needed to get to sleep and get back to Rain Water. I could not get my mind to stop thinking about Drew's arms. They were covered in ink; stains that would never come off. He tried to hide those stains, but all he was doing was keeping himself from coming to God. Once he finally came clean with God, he found out that, in the words of the old hymn, "The blood goes deeper than the stain has gone."

    I was stained like that too. Every sinner was. Maybe not with tattoos, but with things like pride, self-righteousness, disobedience, and many other things. Yet, when God saved me, when He saves any sinner, from that moment forward God sees that sinner as being just as righteous and clean as Jesus Himself.

    What a thought to go to sleep to.

Chapter Seventeen

The voice came with some urgency. "Kyle, Carrie, Aly, wake up, please."

We were instantly wide awake and rising to our feet. We were in the cave again, and it was still dark out.

"I have awakened you a bit earlier in this time period than normal. The need is urgent. You were successful in warning away Rain Water's people yesterday, they have fled into the hills and are safely in hiding. But this has just made the Pit Viper all the angrier, and he is determined to take that wrath out on Rain Water this very day."

"I know why; I know the reason for all of this," Carrie said. "It is about worship, yes, but it is also about a very practical matter. Ever since Drew told me about the Maya Blue, I have had the nagging feeling that it was pretty near the center of all of this.

"After I talked to Drew last, I went and talked to my dad. He has been a rock and mineral collector since he was a kid. I asked him about Maya Blue, and he told me something that ties all of this together.

"Maya blue is made from a certain clay called Palygorskite. It is a magnesium aluminum phyllosilicate that occurs in a type of clay soil common to the Southeastern United States, especially, get this, right here in Georgia.

"A place that it only occurred in limited amounts, though, was in Mexico. In other words, the most essential ingredient of the Itza Mayan worship was eventually found to be running out, and they were looking for more sources of it.

"That explains why they came as far as Georgia and why the Pit Viper has chosen this area to rise and be worshiped.

"It also explains why he intends to wipe out any and all other tribes. Rain Water and his Creeks will not be the last on the list of extermination; if the Pit Viper has his way, he and his Itza Maya will be the only tribe in town, so to speak."

The Conductor nodded in grim understanding. "Then I suggest you get started immediately. You will find that nothing is so powerful as the desire to be worshiped, people will do anything for it. Just ask Lucifer; he could not be satisfied even with being the highest of God's creation; his desire to be worshiped led him to literally try and destroy God Himself. Rain Water will certainly be facing an overwhelming destroying force by nightfall."

We knelt. We prayed. We rose. And then we ran, faster than ever before.

We reached Rain Water's cabin on the mountain about the time that the sun was high in the sky. We threw caution to the wind and burst in, hoping there had been no traps set for us, and hoping our big Indian was still alive. We had to get him out of there, fast, and somewhere into hiding until he could recover and defend himself and his people.

We knew we had another problem, on top of everything else. As always, we only had five days to accomplish our mission, and this was day five. By nightfall, we would be taken back to our time, and Rain Water would be defenseless. We had to get him far away quickly; we had to explain to him who his enemy was and why; we had to give him a fighting chance.

We were relieved to find him alive, and at the same time, we were shocked to find him so very ashen white, trembling, burning up with fever. He was in really bad shape. But as I rushed over to him, Aly, who had taken up watch by the window, shouted in alarm, "Guys, we have a problem!"

She was right. And once again, I knew that had I not been so stubborn during our first few days here, we may not be in this mess. The power of prejudice was as subtle and persuasive as ever, and apparently, I was living proof of that. But now that I knew better, could this disaster be stopped? I looked out the window of the tiny cabin up on the hill and could see movement in the trees down below. The Pit Viper and his posse were headed that way, and if history were a good indicator, they would not be taking any prisoners, including us. From the back of the room, I could hear Rain Water moaning. He was in no shape to fight and no shape to run.

"We have company coming, guys," I said to Carrie and Aly, "and I don't think they're bringing house-warming gifts."

If we were lucky, this would be a very long day. If we were not, we might not live long enough to see tomorrow.

"What do we do, Kyle?" Carrie asked calmly. I knew she was as scared as the rest of us, but was willing herself to be composed. Dad has always taught us that the greatest ally is a composed spirit, and the greatest enemy is panic.

"I don't know, sis. From what I can see, there are fifty, maybe even as many as seventy-five out there. Running is out of the question; Rain Water cannot move on his own, and we cannot carry him fast or far at all. Fighting is also out of the question; that is an overwhelming force heading our way, and we have no weapons.

"I don't really know any other way to say this: all we can do is pray, then find whatever we can use as weapons and just do the best we can."

I expected my sisters to cry; after all, I had basically just told them that we were all likely to die in the next little bit. Somehow, after all, we have been through together, I guess I should have known them better than that.

"Then quit yapping and start praying, please, so we can get something to whack people with," Aly said defiantly. "I got dibs on the pointy headed dude."

I looked at Carrie, and she had the same look on her face that Aly had on hers. I shook my head in amazement, smiled, we all knelt, and I began to pray.

"Lord, You have called us to this task, this place, and this hour. Lord, we have so often fought, schemed, and worked to win the battles You have placed before us, and we gratefully acknowledge You as the source of all of our strength and the author of all of our victories.

"But Lord, we now face a force that is greater than any strength we possess, and we find ourselves in a position where no scheming on our part can turn the tide. Lord, the best way I know how to say it, we need a miracle here.

"Lord, for the sake of this man and for the sake of His people, please help us. I don't know what to ask for because I don't know what will work. But I know that you are both all-knowing enough to see our desperate need and all powerful enough to meet it.

"Help us, Lord, in Jesus name we pray, amen."

Still kneeling, we all lifted our heads and looked eye to eye. An unspoken understanding passed between us, we rose up, hugged each other tightly, and I really didn't want to let go. These two girls, my sisters, were my best friends in the world, and I just hoped that if I died today, I could at least keep them alive in so doing.

But, with Aly, no tender moment lasts very long.

"Okay," she said perfunctorily, "now to find something to whack, poke, slice, or clobber with. Carrie, I assume that you will want the bow and three remaining arrows. I will use this," and as she said that she picked up the old rustic chair, smashed it to the ground, and picked up a leg of it. "This should give out several nasty head knots and maybe a broken bone or two. After that, I will just kick, claw, bite, and in general, be somebody's worst nightmare as long as I have breath in my body. If I have to go to heaven today, I intend to do so with a lot of somebody else's busted teeth in hand."

"Nice, Squirt, very nice. I will take this other chair leg, and hopefully I can do a great impersonation of Samson swinging that dead donkey's jawbone. Carrie, you make those three arrows count and then get behind us."

"On it, bro, already on it," she said as she put an arrow to the string and broke out the window to make ready.

The Pit Viper and his posse did not waste time. They came just out of the trees and hailed the cabin.

"Your time is up, young trouble-makers, you and your injured Indian friend. But I am a kind and merciful god; all I require of you is to drag Rain Water out to me, and I will let you three go free. This is not your fight; you do not need to die today."

"You are not a God at all!" Carrie shouted as she swung into view of the window and let her first arrow fly with a vengeance.

The Pit Viper was as fast as the snake he was named for, and it was a good thing for him. Had he not ducked, Carrie's shot would have dead-centered his chest. As it was, when he dropped down, it nailed the guy behind him in the shoulder.

The posse scattered for the trees and every one of them got behind one, or a bush, or a rock, for cover. They did not know how many arrows we had; that might just buy us some time.

Or not.

The next thing I knew the cabin was getting the "thunk thunk thunk thunk thunk" treatment as a barrage of arrows came whizzing our way. Several of them sailed right in through the window and sunk into the back wall. The thunk thunk thunks were mixed in with the sound of sporadic rifle fire as well; they had come loaded for bear with everything they had.

Carrie let fly with her remaining two arrows. Aly and I dove for the back wall, yanked out several of the arrows the posse had shot in after us, and tossed them to Carrie, who let fly with every one of them.

She ducked again as another barrage came sailing in, and as she did she shouted, "I hit two more of them!"

The Pit Viper was no fool. He had watched carefully from behind a tree, as I thought he might, and he realized that we only had one shooter and that we did not have any arrows of our own left.

"Charge them!" he screamed. "Do it now!"

I heard the posse let out a war whoop as they broke from cover and rushed our way.

Carrie screamed and dove behind Aly and me. We braced ourselves; I estimated it would take them about five seconds to close the gap from the trees to the front door. This was it, it was really it, we were going to die in a matter of seconds.

I prayed. Quickly. What for? The trumpet. If God would just come back this very second and rapture us, we would not have to die. But then I thought (and all of this raced through my head in just a split second or less) "I guess that is impossible, because if the rapture happens now, there will never be a future, and we wouldn't even have been alive to be here!"

The trumpet did not sound.

But another sound did happen, a big sound. Another war whoop, followed by a mass "whooshing" of arrows, and then the sound of a massive body of people slamming violently into other people.

Not knowing what was happening, I instinctively grabbed my sisters and shoved them into the back corner of the room and covered them with my body.

The conflict outside raged, violently, for another few minutes and then everything fell silent.

The front door opened.

The sun was behind the figure that stood in the doorway, making him a perfect silhouette. That prevented me from seeing his face; he was merely a shadow, an outline, but I could tell by the headdress that it was an Indian, a warrior.

I rose and faced him, ready to kill or die.

And then I jumped as the figure moved like lightning, and a "whoosh" came by my ear.

I heard the knife slam into the wall just behind me. I whirled and looked at it.

I knew that knife.

"Hello, white warrior, have you missed me?"

I didn't just know the knife; I knew the voice as well. I just couldn't believe it was really real.

"Black Crow? But how, why?"

He stepped out of the light and into the room where I could see him. His face still held nearly as much hatred for me as when I defeated him in Rogersville and thus deprived him of the chance to be chief[1], but it now held something else as well, a bit of maturity, perhaps.

"My brother, Chief Falling Rain, saw your smoke signal asking for help five days ago in the early morning. He immediately sent me and our best warriors here to find and help you. Once we arrived, we had no trouble following your tracks in the hills, yours and the tracks of those that hunted you."

I just stood there, dumbfounded, trying to figure out what he meant. Smoke signal asking for help? What smoke signal? And then it clicked:

For some reason, I turned to look back toward the cave that we had left a few hundred yards behind us. When I did, I noticed smoke rising through a fissure in the rock, and drifting oh, so high into the sky.

"Guys, we're forgetting mom and dad's rule. Someone didn't turn the light off before we left," I said as I pointed back toward the cave.

"I got this, bro," Aly said. Immediately there were pine needles and dirt flying out from under her feet as she raced back up the path. In three or four minutes, the torch had been

---

[1] You can read about this in book four of the Night Heroes series, "The Blade of Black Crow."

extinguished, she was back with us, and we were once again headed down the mountain.

Could it be? Could God have used that torch, and Aly putting it out, to send out a smoke signal for help, one that could be seen by our friends so very far away in Rogersville, Tennessee? That would be nothing short of a miracle, or, as my dad would put it, "About what you would expect from God."

I just shook my head in amazement and slowly dipped my head in a show of thanks and respect for Black Crow.

"Thank you, great warrior of the Creek Indians. Thank you for coming to our aid and also the aid of one of your own."

I motioned to Rain Water. Black Crow went to him, knelt beside him, and looked at his wound.

"Did you tend to his wound and take care of him?"

"Yes, Black Crow, I did,"

He nodded approvingly. "You did well, for a white man. It is I who owe you thanks. We will tend to him; we will see that he fully recovers, and we will help his people here as long as they need.

"Their enemies and yours, in this case, will not be a problem. Dead people rarely are."

I nodded in respect again. I knew that Black Crow and his people were more than a match for the Pit Viper and his posse. The Pit

Viper had come to this land expecting to be a god; all he had gotten was an unexpected trip into eternity to meet the real God.

Black Crow and his people gathered up Rain Water and prepared to leave. They would be far more at home in the trees than in this cabin as they took the time to tend to our big Indian. Rain Water lifted his head as they began to carry him out, and motioned for them to stop in front of me. Then he spoke, oh, so weakly:

"Thank you, young man. On behalf of my people and me, thank you."

I smiled, took his hand in mine, and spoke back. "You are quite welcome, my friend, but you owe me very little thanks. The real thanks belongs to the God who knows how to summon help for us before we even know we need it, and who can change the hearts of people like me who are often too stubborn to see past their own prejudices. Be blessed, my friend, and may Jesus, the Great Spirit, ever walk with you.

Epilog and Historical Information

The information on Maya Blue is historically correct. It was used to paint sacrifices in Mayan worship, and it was made from palygorskite, a kind of fuller's earth. Recent discoveries have led to a debate in the historical/archaeological community. Some hold to the view that the Mayan's never got far beyond Mexico. Others point to old mound structures in and around Hiawassee and the identical chemical composition of Maya Blue found in both Georgia and Mexico as evidence that the Mayans made their way all the way into Georgia at some point.

The reason the Pit Viper had a pointed head is because the Mayans used wedge shape boards to force their baby's heads into an odd shape while their heads were still soft and growing. They believed it gave them a more fierce appearance.

Coming Soon

The Mothman

My breath was coming in gasps, and I could feel the tears stinging my eyes as I ran, panicked, through the pitch black West Virginia night. There was no use telling me that there is no such thing as the Mothman. Yesterday I would have agreed with you, but now I could not shake him, nor could I find Kyle or Aly, and I knew I was going to die…

Other Books in the Night Heroes Series

Cry From the Coal Mine

Free Fall

Broken Brotherhood

The Blade of Black Crow

Ghost Ship

Other Books by Dr. Wagner

From Footers to Finish Nails

Beyond the Colored Coat

Daniel: Breathtaking

Esther: Five Feasts and the Fingerprints of God

Nehemiah: A Labor of Love

Marriage Makers/Marriage Breakers

I'm Saved! Now What???

Don't Muzzle the Ox

www.ingramcontent.com/pod-product-compliance
Lightning Source LLC
Chambersburg PA
CBHW050736230626
47052CB00002BA/396

*9 7 8 1 9 4 1 0 3 9 9 8 4 *